CURSED
PRINCESS
CLUB
LambCat

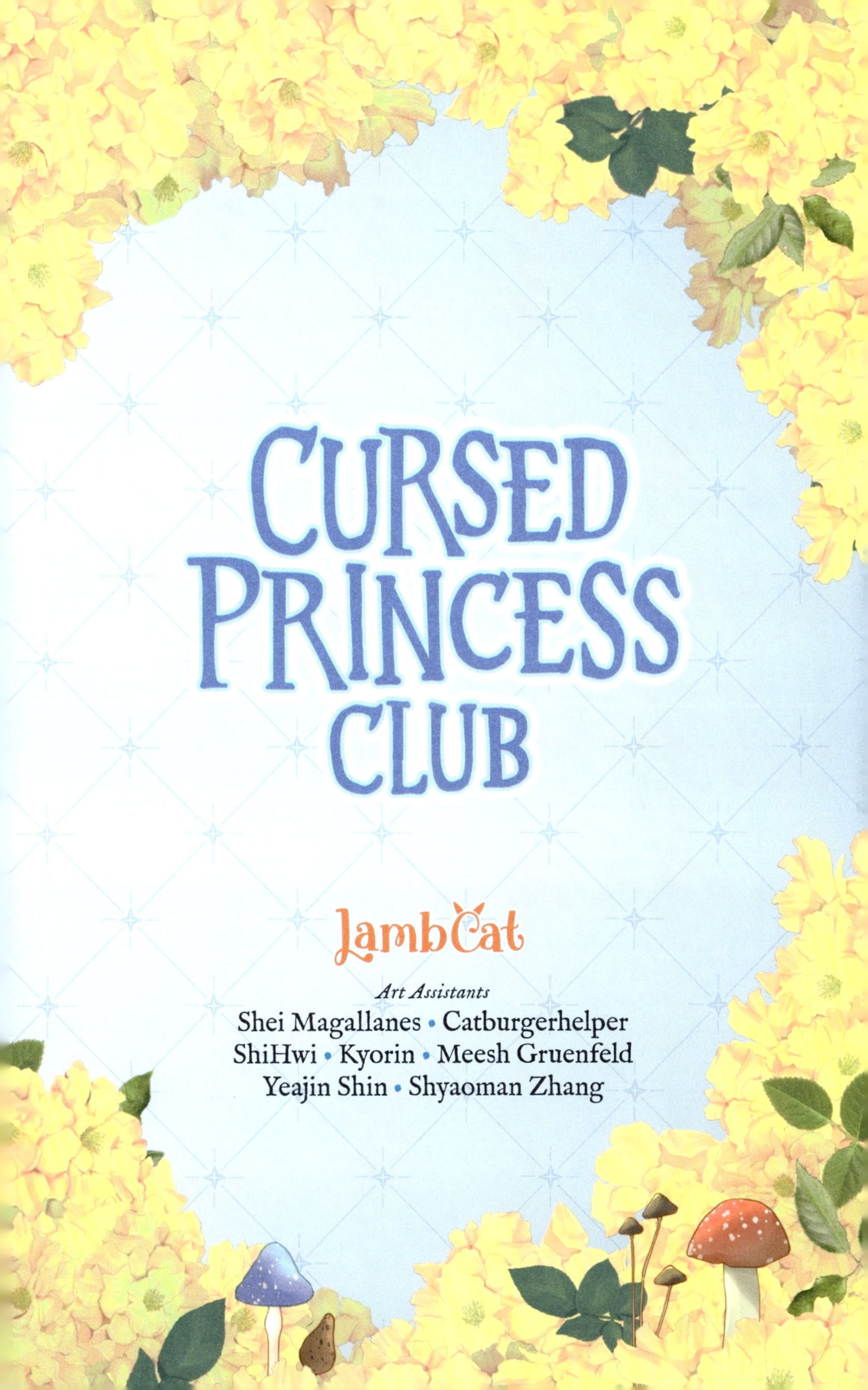

CURSED PRINCESS CLUB

LambCat

Art Assistants

Shei Magallanes • Catburgerhelper
ShiHwi • Kyorin • Meesh Gruenfeld
Yeajin Shin • Shyaoman Zhang

Published in Canada by WEBTOON Unscrolled, a division of Wattpad WEBTOON Studios, Inc.
36 Wellington Street E., Suite 200. Toronto, ON M5E 1C7
The digital version of Cursed Princess Club was originally published on WEBTOON.com in 2019.

www.WEBTOONUnscrolled.com

First WEBTOON Unscrolled edition: January 2024
ISBN: 978-1-99077-888-9 (Hardcover) ISBN 978-1-99077-887-2 (Paperback)

Library and Archives Canada Cataloging in Publication information is available upon request.
Printed and bound in Canada
3 5 7 9 10 8 6 4
WEBTOON UNSCROLLED™

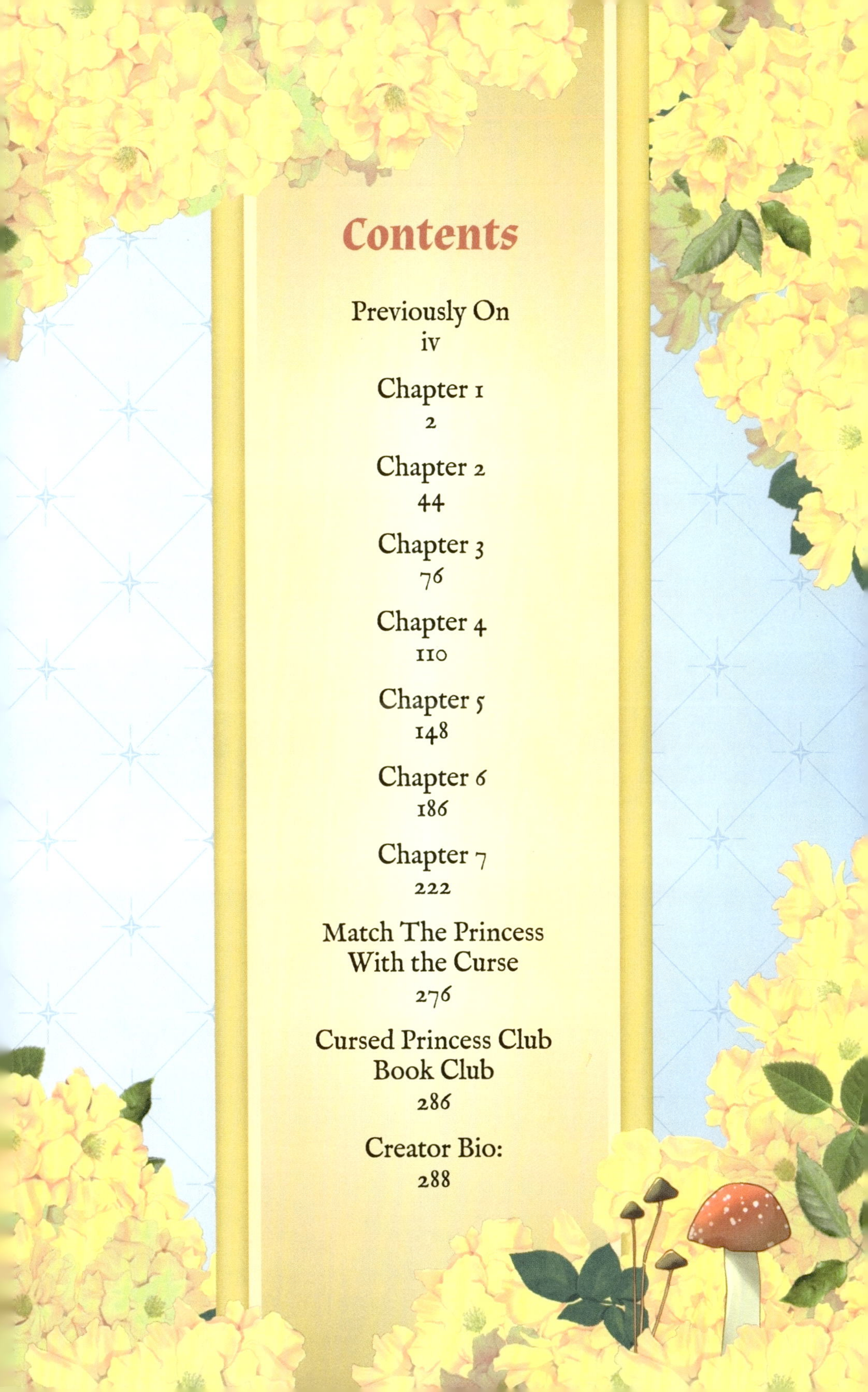

Contents

Frightened by the terrifying, cracked reflection she keeps encountering, Gwen attempts to fix it by asking the Cursed Princess Club to teach her how to be beautiful.

Prez advises her that the solution isn't found in endlessly gazing at her reflection for answers, but in learning to love herself.

Jealous of Gwen, Aurelia tricks her into entering the forbidden barn. Inside, Gwen flees from a horrifyingly giant spider, only to discover that it's Prez in her cursed form! Enraged by Aurelia's actions, Prez chooses to banish her from the club.

Prez then recounts the tale of how she unintentionally killed the man who cursed her, Prince Whitney.

Meanwhile, each of the Pastel Princesses continues to grow closer to their betrothed Plaid Princes, including Gwen and Frederick.

However, Frederick grapples with internal conflicts, questioning his desires and whether he truly deserves Gwen, especially when a new rival arrives who believes **he** does.

Chapter
1

Outside the castle of the Pastel Kingdom...

Naked prince to your left! Quick, grab him!

Wheee–!

Ow, my pelvis...

Hello again, Princess Gwendolyn...

...Um, did you just crawl out of those bushes?

Oh, I went to visit a friend– **I-I MEAN...!**
Er, then I remembered that, um...I don't have any!
Whew...I'm so startled by everything that I almost revealed the Cursed Princess Club...!!

S-so what brings you to our palace?
rustle
Oh! Well, it's to—

Ah, Lord Leopold! Nice to see you!
And how sweet of you to bring flowers. I adore them!
grab
O-oh, of course, Your Majesty. Um...is this a bad time...?
Haha, why, whatever are you talking about?! You mean what's going on over there?
My girls are just having a bit of a tantrum. Teenagers, am I right?
AAAHHH!!!
It's **not** a tantrum! We're all **protesting**!!! Gwen and Jamie too!
And none of us are going inside until you accept our demands to stop locking us up in the palace!!

Gwennie-pie, I can't believe they dragged you out here as well...
You're sweet to come and greet our guest...
...but you need to go back inside! You're breaking Papa's decrees!
The same thing goes for your older sisters...!
STOMP
STOMP!
Maria! Lorena! Stop this outlandish behavior right now!
We have a **guest**! Have you no decorum?!
Well, maybe you should focus on stopping the butt-naked one first, then, hmm?
...Fair point.
GUARDS!!!

Why is it taking you buffoons so long to capture my son?!

H-his skin...so **smooth**...It melts right through your fingers, Your Majesty...
wheeze
pant
cough
It's like trying to grab a buttered noodle...

Well then, grab a colander and get back to **work**!!
YES, YOUR MAJESTY!!
dash–!

HEY! What did I say about looking toward my daughters, though?!!
Cover your faces!!
R-right!! Sorry! Uhhh...
step
step
step

SLAM!
AGH—

THUD!
Wahoo—
Ughhh...
I don't think I can win this...

It's hard to juggle being a single parent while holding down the job...
of ruling a kingdom and leading expeditions!
sniffle
The only time I get to see my babies is when I say good morning, and then it's off to work!
How can I possibly keep you safe if I let you leave the palace?!!

But if it means that you're all going to protest against Papa, then...
Fine. I give in.
Gasp!
R-really?! We won...?!

Well, yes...But there must be compromises for your safety.
We'll have to sit down and hash out some new rules first...!
You can't stay out too late! And you still can't leave when I'm gone on expeditions...
And you'll need a chaperone if you go outside, like Miss Agatha or Molly or—

Or the Plaid Princes?

...I suppose...

What if they're all busy and we wanna go somewhere?

Well, you'll simply have to wait! Or...

...I suppose we can arrange for one of the guards to escort you!
Gotcha!!—
rustle
pant

WAIT, WHAT DID HE SAY?!!
Riip-
...That's coming out of your paycheck, mate.

...So should we take his offer?
I mean...it's probably the best outcome we're ever gonna get.

Okay, it's decided then...
Father, we have a deal!
SHAKE!
Good. Now that that's settled...

...everyone stop ganging up on Papa and **GET INSIDE THE PALACE!!!**
Y-yes, Father...

YOU TOO, BUDDY!!!
—Er, I mean...
You too, buddy–! Come on in...!
Hehe.

So, Gwendolyn...
to answer your question, the reason I am here is—

So when we were at Lance's birthday party recently...

and we got our portrait painted with that inebriated celebrity cow you kids loved so much...

...I was hoping to poach their artist.

But just like every other time we've had our family portrait painted...

Live. Laugh. Laverne.

...there was something lacking in the craftsmanship that I just couldn't put my finger on.

Tsk...

Disgraceful. Let me fix this for you, Your Majesty.

...Uhh, who are you?

Here you are.
Oh, my word!!!

This is it! This is my baby girl!
I don't know what was missing before, but you fixed it!

Oh, that's easy, Your Majesty.
Talent. **Talent** was missing.
Go eat paint, Leopold...!
I-quit...

It was absolute serendipity!
So I hired Leopold to come here today to start on a new project, which is...

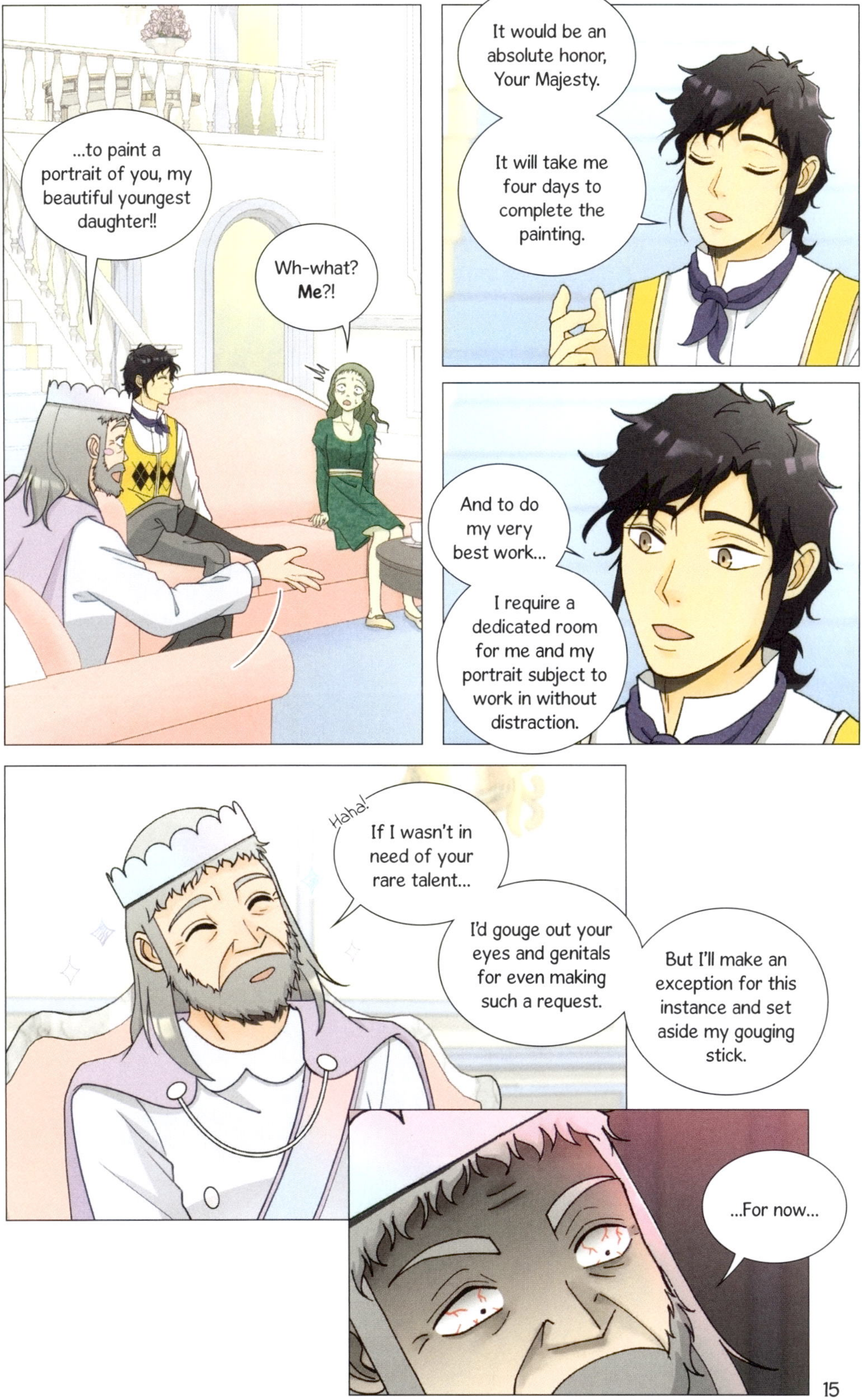

Haha!

If I wasn't in need of your rare talent...

I'd gouge out your eyes and genitals for even making such a request.

But I'll make an exception for this instance and set aside my gouging stick.

...For now...

Good, Jamie!!! You were amazing out there!!

pat

Have another cookie!

...

chomp
chomp

close
Well, then...
Shall we begin,
Gwendolyn?
rustle
rustle

A portrait of just **me**?! Why does Papa want this?
I feel so nervous, even though I never do for our family portraits...

What's this feeling again...
It seems familiar...

M-my reflection...
...it's shattered again?!!

Wait...
The hole seems smaller this time.
And so do the cracks...
but why is it happening again?!

CREAK~
step
step
step
Ugh...

Thank you, Bart. You can set those down next to me.
Oh! I can help carry painting supplies!

That's very kind, Gwendolyn. But Bart hates when I try to assist him.
"You can pry these boxes from my cold, dead hands," he always says—

Hello~
—Ah!!
Wh-where did Gwendolyn go?!

Oh, she's helping your butler, Bart.
You can pry these boxes from my cold, dead hands.
Please, pry them... My fingers have poor circulation, and they won't move.

Wait, you're the prince from outside! The naked one with no shame.
I believe I remember you from the party at the Plaid Kingdom as well...

You were the one who recklessly blinded everyone with your flashy entrance...
Shine~!

I was trying to get Gwennie's attention as she was standing alone.

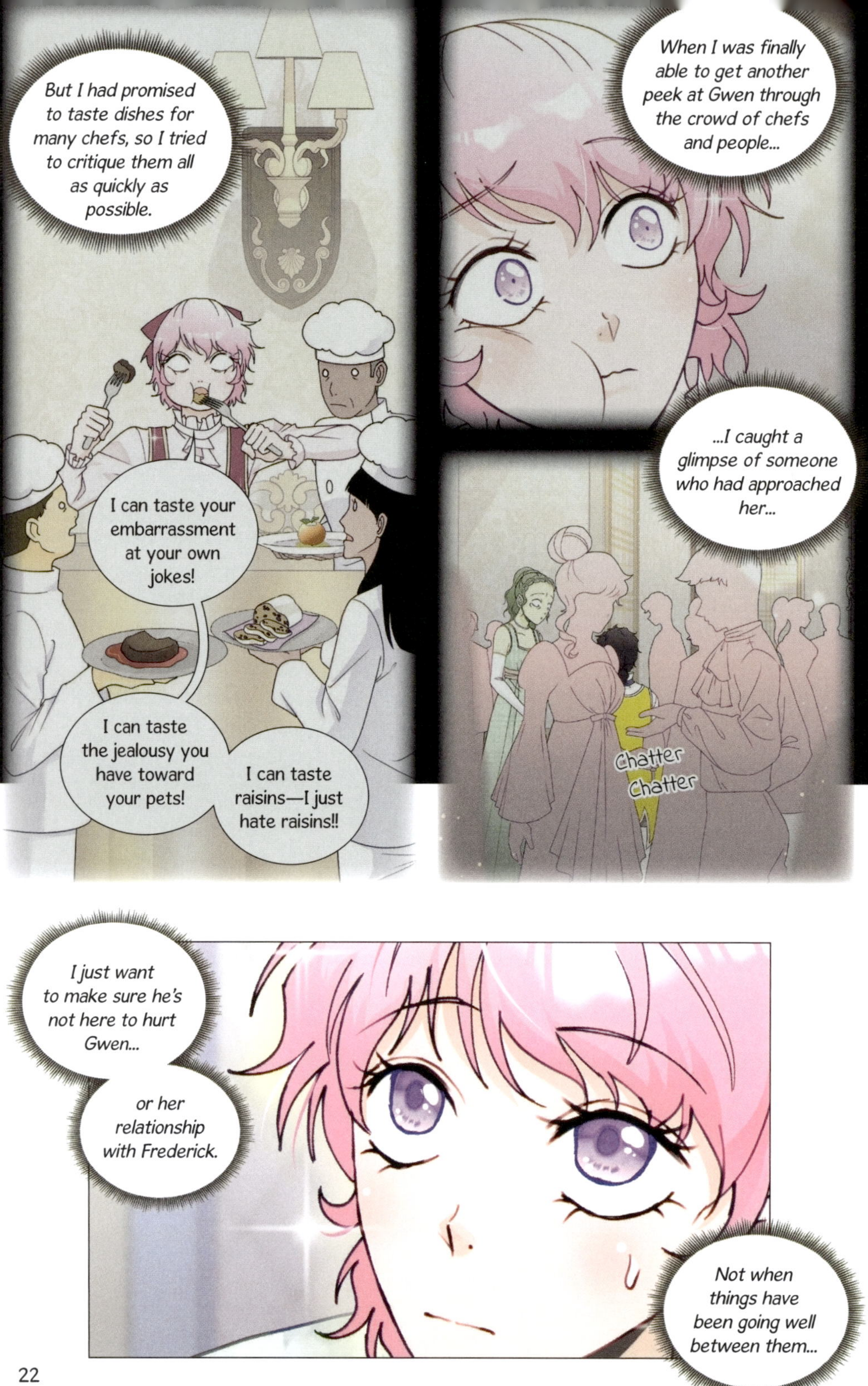

But I had promised to taste dishes for many chefs, so I tried to critique them all as quickly as possible.

I can taste your embarrassment at your own jokes!

I can taste the jealousy you have toward your pets!

I can taste raisins—I just hate raisins!!

When I was finally able to get another peek at Gwen through the crowd of chefs and people...

...I caught a glimpse of someone who had approached her...

Chatter Chatter

Oh, I thought I'd just check in from time to time to see how you guys are doing.
Y'know, to make sure you're not, um..."coloring outside any lines"...
Coloring outside any lines?!
How dare you suggest I need micromanaging! I'm a **freaking art prodigy**!!
N-no, it's a metaphor—
I don't need that kind of negative energy polluting my workspace!
So please leave and allow me to work in peace!
Um, but... o-okay...
And kindly take your excessive sparkles with you!!
Swat
gather

Okay...I believe we're ready to begin now.

I must state again how delighted I am for the opportunity...

...to paint a portrait of someone as beautiful as you.

Prez taught me how to make them disappear...

Gwen, all you have to do...

is love yourself. Exactly the way you are.

Until that day, you have to lean more on those of us around you who love you.

Since then, I **have** been leaning on the support of friends and family.

And it helped. The cracks disappeared.

But the mirror shows that when they're not around...

...I still don't have much love for myself.

Oh, well, I see you're as modest as you are gorgeous.

not paying attention

But you needn't be with me.

People always think that my life must be grand as a young and brilliantly successful artist.

Every day, I get to paint models and celebrities that society deems the most beautiful.

I see it differently, though.

I **do** take great pride in my craft.

I view my job much like being a wine connoisseur but with people's faces.

But to be frankly callous...

I find most of society's tastes in beauty utterly boring.

They prefer nothing but the same type of predictably sweet flavors over and over again...
always lacking any distinct characteristics.
Just how dull can their palates be?!
But when I spotted you from the balcony at the Plaid Kingdom party...
it was like happening upon a rare, fine wine.
There's a complexity to your beauty...
that challenges those who gaze at you with depth and uniqueness...
You bought Blaine merch?!
...Sooo is this like an exorcism before-and-after portrait or something...?
...a uniqueness that many people and artists wouldn't be able to appreciate immediately due to their simple biases.

I knew I had to find my way to you no matter the cost.
And here we are now...!
still not paying attention

I've been selfish...
...relying too much on my friends and family for my self-esteem.

What do I need to do to get past that...?
I wish I knew...

...So I'm relieved to hear that my advances aren't unwelcome...

step
step
...because I may be here as your portrait artist, but...

...I want to
be more than
that for you,
Gwendolyn.
...R-really?
Yes...
Anything you
want...

...Can you teach me how to love and accept myself?

...Huh?
I did say "anything," but...
I kind of meant it romantically, not as, like, a life coach...

I've been relying too much on my friends and family to love myself...
instead of learning to accept what I see in the mirror all on my own.

Wait...Do you not think you're beautiful?

Um...I guess I used to. My family has always told me I am.
But...I've since learned otherwise.

I do believe that when my friends and family tell me I'm beautiful...
they're saying it out of kindness and because they care about my well-being.

Oh! Well then, does it perhaps make you feel better to know that...
my words to you were meant without any kindness or hope for your well-being whatsoever?

...Hmm... No, I guess not.

Sigh
Okay, I'll help.
I suppose one can only accept love from others...
to the degree that they allow it within themselves...

step
step
step
...so a few trite words couldn't hurt.

Besides, as much as I despise when a good mood gets spoiled...

tie

...I despise it much more when...

people hold an inaccurate sense of beauty about themselves due to society!

Now...
pardon my tone, Your Highness...
...but I implore you to take this time to sit...
and start to be more appreciative of all the things that make you who you are!

...!

For if you wish to stop relying on your friends and family...
then the first step is to truly believe what they say to you.

To choose to let the uninformed opinion of some idiots invalidate them...
is nothing but an **insult** to your loved ones.
And also to me, which is the greatest offense.

Oh...I never saw it that way...

Tell me, Gwendolyn. What is your favorite food?
Um, I love apple pie...

Well, what if I told you that apple pie and all manner of sweet foods disgust me to no end?
Would apple pie now become disgusting to you, knowing how I feel?

Um...no...I'd still love it the same.

Exactly.
So I don't know who or what made you question your appearance...
but I guess I would say to them...

..."Good. More for me..."

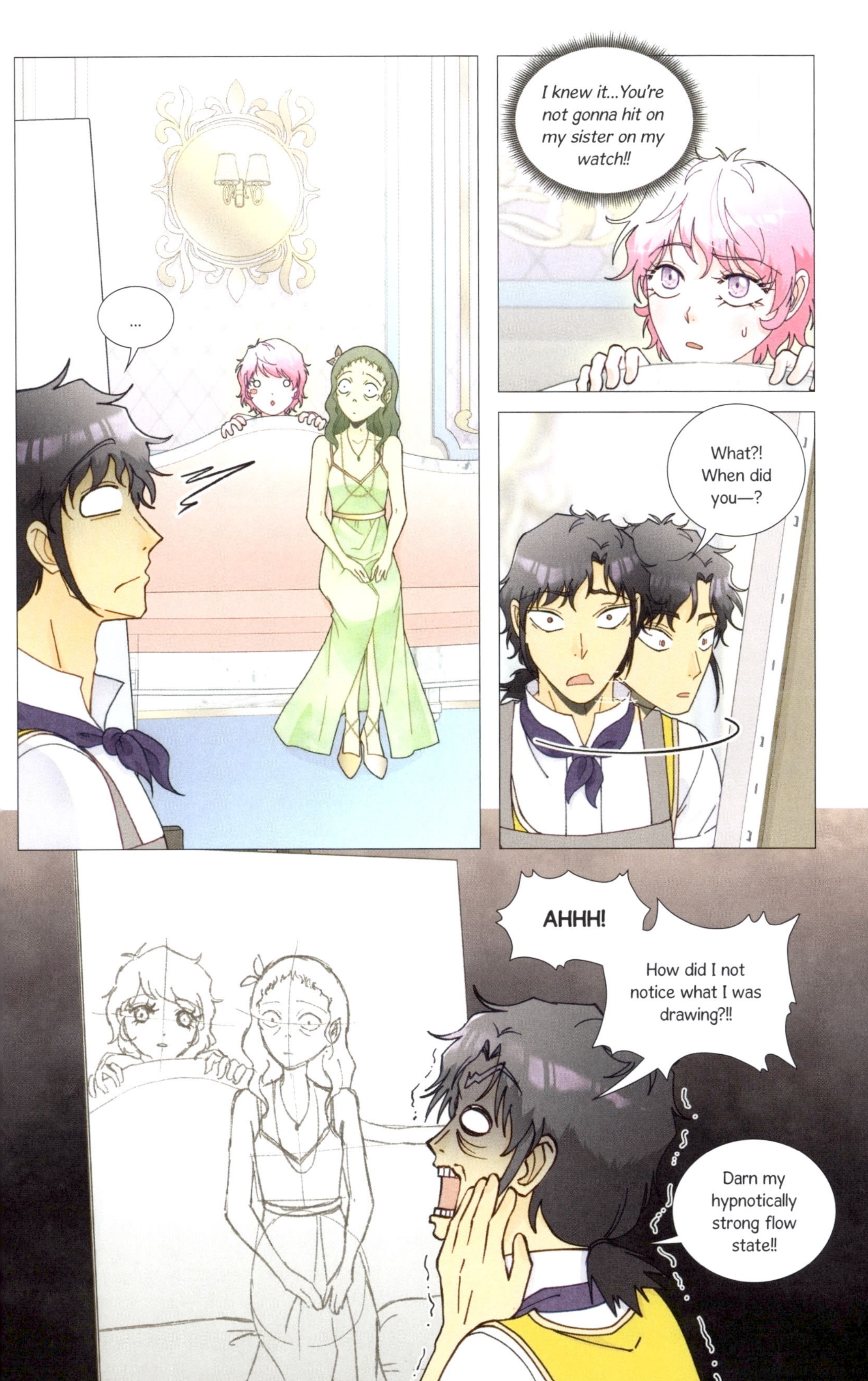
...
I knew it...You're not gonna hit on my sister on my watch!!
What?! When did you—?
AHHH!
How did I not notice what I was drawing?!!
Darn my hypnotically strong flow state!!

How **dare** you tarnish this painting! I have to start all over now!!
splatter
I know what you're doing!! You think just because you have flashy, shiny looks that the public adores...
you deserve to be the star of **every** portrait!

N-no, that's not what—
Well, you're **not** getting in this one!!
I told your sister that I despise it when people hold an inaccurate sense of beauty about themselves due to society.
And that applies to you as well!

Most other people might be dazzled by your superficial looks, but not me.
If Gwendolyn's looks are like a rare, fine wine in my eyes...
then you are like...

...a **sickeningly sweet syrup**. Just...
...HIDEOUS.

SICKENINGLY SWEET
HIDEOUS
...
This **was** about my sister...
but now it's **personal**.

mumble
...Oh. I see.

mumble
mumble
...Well, I'll make sure this hideous face forever haunts your portraits...

...and your dreams...

...Wh- where did he go...?
...

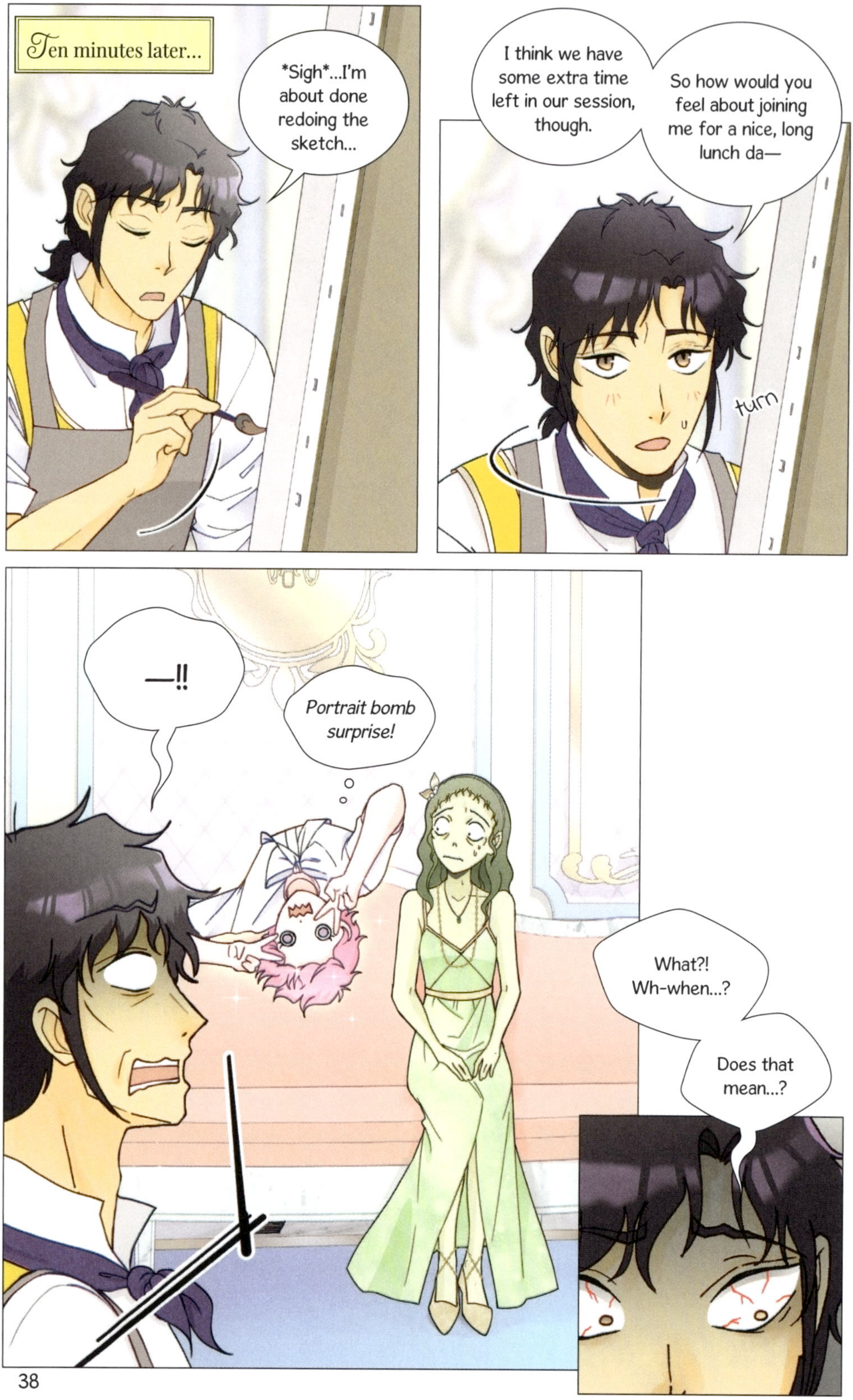

—!!

Portrait bomb surprise!

What?! Wh-when...?

Does that mean...?

NOOOO!!!!
HOW DID THIS HAPPEN AGAIN?!
BEGONE!!!
toss

Another ten minutes later...
turn
Okay, I'm done again. H-how about a brief picnic?
AAAH!!!

Ten minutes after that...
J-just a light snack?

Ten minutes again...
#$%^@!!
Crack!!..

Chapter 2

The next morning in the not-so-distant Plaid Kingdom...
chirp
chirp
Good morning, everyone.
As you know, I've been taking my gala committee responsibilities extremely seriously this year.
And even though you sometimes roll your eyes at me for it...
Ahem, Frederick...
clink
chew
I will bestow this gift upon you, my brothers.
Whoa...isn't this the super-posh gala that happens once every five years?
It's this autumn, huh?
That's right... Now let's go invite the princesses.
The 32nd Pentennial
Bippity Bop
Live music | Champagne bar | Luxury clowns
ADMIT ONE

Well, I personally despise that gaudy event.

But I can't say it won't be a memorable experience for you and your fiancés.

Blaine got us tickets too. Will you accompany me, my beautiful queen?
Depends. Who's catering?
Oh...Well, I don't know...

Let's go and visit the Pastel Princesses today and invite them to the gala!
Okay!

Oh, I should also tell you boys some interesting news from the Pastel King involving his daughters.
It turns out the princesses staged a coup against him...
and he's finally allowing them to go outside their palace more often now.

...

Heh, my dear friend Jack has such dumb rules about parenthood.

Frederick!!
You didn't pass the butter dish to your right after you used it, you classless heathen!
You know the rules! Thirty push-ups!!

munch
sigh
Yes, Father...

Anyhow, I also heard that the youngest daughter, Gwendolyn...
is getting her portrait painted by a young lord from one of those insufferable kingdoms.
What was his name again? Leonard? Lerman?

LEOPOLD!
HUH?!!
Slip
That's right. Lord Leopold of the Argyle Kingdom.

Would you like to come with me, Gwendolyn?

...What **can** I do...?

...What do I even **want** to do...?

What are you boys talking about?

I leave that bagel up there as a daily reminder of the error of my ways as a father.

I won't control Frederick any longer. He is free to pursue whomever and whatever he wants.

Do what makes you happy, son. That's my new motto.

...S-sorry, what...?

You can't be serious, Father...

freeze-

I'm quite serious.

Let Frederick be, boys.

Was Father really serious about what he said...?

...That he's not enforcing my engagement to Gwen anymore...?

Actually, at Lance's party, Gwen also seemed to believe our engagement was called off...

Wait...Are you going to marry Gwendolyn?

HUH?!!!

W-well, umm...

No.

...What...?

Don't worry, Frederick.
It's okay. I haven't forgotten what we talked about in the hallway of our palace about just being friends.
If that's all true, then...
I guess my wish came true when I stood up to Father last time...
W-with all due respect, Father...
...I refuse to marry Gwendolyn!!!

...And that means I don't really have to do anything now.
I can just have more time to read and relax.

...
THE DOGYSS

...I don't feel like relaxing though. I feel...restless.
...Is this not what I wanted?

Do I...
Do I miss Gwen...?
...As my friend?...Or something else?

It's kinda hard to tell when I've never had friends before...

What am I supposed to do?

Frederick, if there's something you really want, you have to go after it!!!

It seems easy enough in theory...
I always know what other people want of me.
And I seem to know what I want other people to think of me, but...
What I want...? Why is it so hard for me to figure that out?!

What am I saying?...
I know why...

I know there are things I truly want and like deep down...
once I say them out loud...

...they'll get torn apart.

...!
But if I just sit here...
grab
...
...that means I don't get to see her again...
All I know for now...
step
step
step
...is that I don't want that!

It's okay, son. I foresaw this happening.

I'm proud of you for coming to your senses.

So don't worry. I've prepared just the thing for you...

You'll have to assemble it yourself. Shouldn't be too hard, though.

Íĺämäkärţ

slap

...O-okay...

Better get to it. Clock's ticking, daylight's fading!

step

step

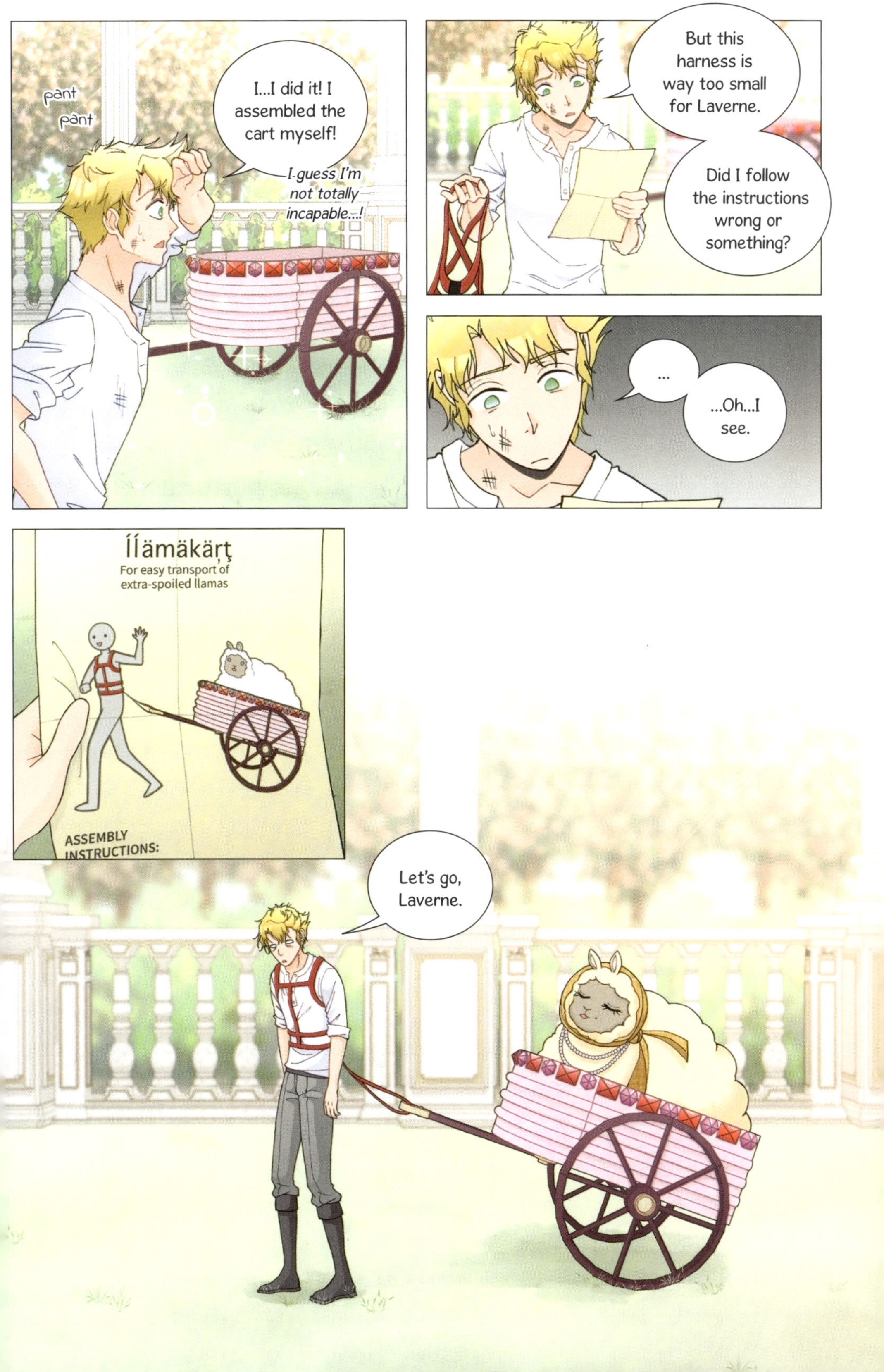

Íĺämäkärț
For easy transport of extra-spoiled llamas
ASSEMBLY INSTRUCTIONS:

Let's go, Laverne.

Clop
Clop
Clop
Can you believe what happened yesterday?!
At first, I was disappointed in the king for caving to the princesses' demands.
He was right to keep them safe within the palace walls!
They're too pure to be exposed to all the indecency that lurks outside!
But once again, His Majesty was wise beyond my comprehension!
The princesses **do** deserve to see and experience the world!
They just need someone to guide them safely through it!
Mate, hold up—

Didn't you hear?!

That means we'll get a chance to escort the princesses one day!!

Y-yeah, mate, I heard. But—

I'm going to get to walk alongside Maria...

maybe talk to her, a-and if I'm lucky, I'll even get to—

Ogle her, right?!

I know what you're thinking, you filthy, standing mongoose of a guard.

Hi again–

Gasp

Th-the Plaid Princes!

Wait...
Sorry, what?
But...
then how do you guard them?
That doesn't seem like a very good policy...

Besides...
you're the shallow one who only likes her for her perfect looks!

...

That's right. I'm shallow...
and so are all the things I like about Princess Maria.

And you know what?
I like them **SO much** that I'm gonna tell you everything you're missing out on, Lieutenant **Dandruff.**
H-huh? It's **Dander**! I mean, **Dandridge**!

You'll never see how beautiful her eyes are and how they shine bigger and brighter than the largest ocean...
GRAB
H-hey, I don't wanna hear this...!

And you'll never feel the softness of her hair...
and how it wafts like a gentle spring meadow wrapped with ribbon...
Stop!!! You're being really mean—!

And my favorite thing is how she smells...
like birdseed with a hint of slightly damp forest creatures...
...

Blaine, Lance!! What a wonderful surprise! Please come in!
Oh, good afternoon, Your Highnesses!
drop
AH—

Until next time, gentlemen.
step
step

step
step
step

I can't believe it. We get to see the princes practically any time we want now...
We can finally go on dates without always having a parent hovering over us—
Parent...

I don't want any of you here.
I don't approve of any of this arranged marriage nonsense.

Their mom hates us...
I haven't told anyone. I didn't want to worry Lorena or Gwen...

...and I don't really want to bring it up with Blaine if I can help it.
Does he know how his mother feels?
Is there something I can do to change her mind?

Knock
Knock
Yes, come in.

Sorry to interrupt...
but look! The Plaid Princes stopped by to congratulate us on our newfound freedom!
Hello, Lord Leopold...

Oh! Where's Frederick? Is he running late again?
Uhh, h-he heard Gwen was having her portrait painted and didn't want to interrupt...!
B-but he sends his regards, Gwen!

O-oh, yes, of course...
Um, please tell him I say hello as well.

So do you think you'll be done soon enough to join us for a trip into town?

Um, no. I think we're actually a bit behind schedule on the portrait.
Thanks to a certain, sparkly someone.
I also have to attend my extracurricular study later this afternoon.

Oh, right! I guess you get to see the outside world regularly anyway!
Though school isn't a part of the world I'd ever want to visit...
Okay, I guess we'll see you later this evening!
Father's new decrees don't let us stay out too late on dates...
Bye! Have fun!

step
step
step
All right!
Let's go somewhere you've always wanted to visit, Lorena!
I wanna watch a fight!!
Best fiancé ever...
And how about you, Maria?
We can go anywhere on our own.
Oh! Um, well, I was wondering...
D-does your mother like any particular jewelry, Blaine?
step
step
Hmm, I believe she's partial to charm bracelets...
Fantastic! Then I would like to go shopping!!

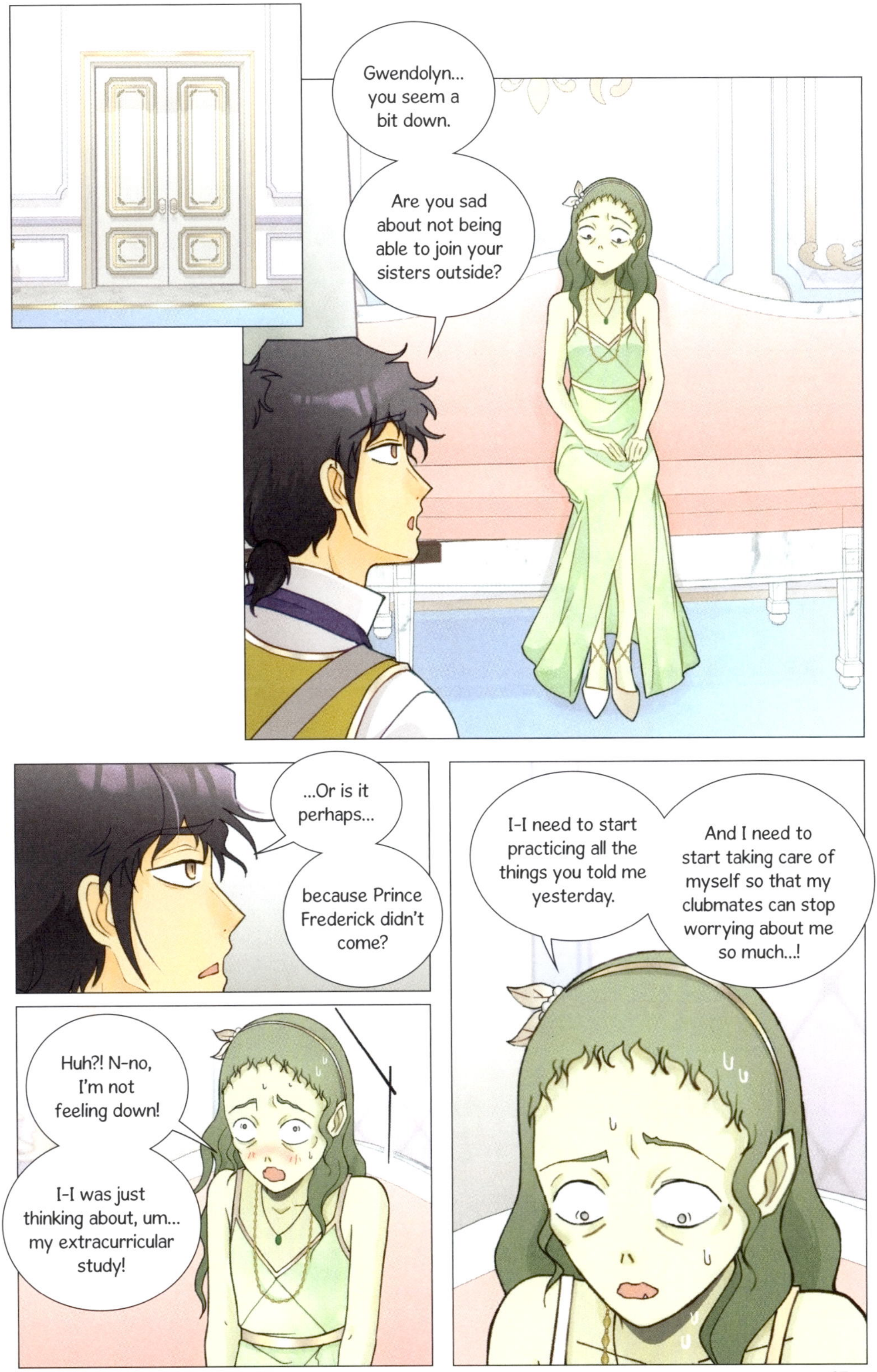

Gwendolyn... you seem a bit down.

Are you sad about not being able to join your sisters outside?

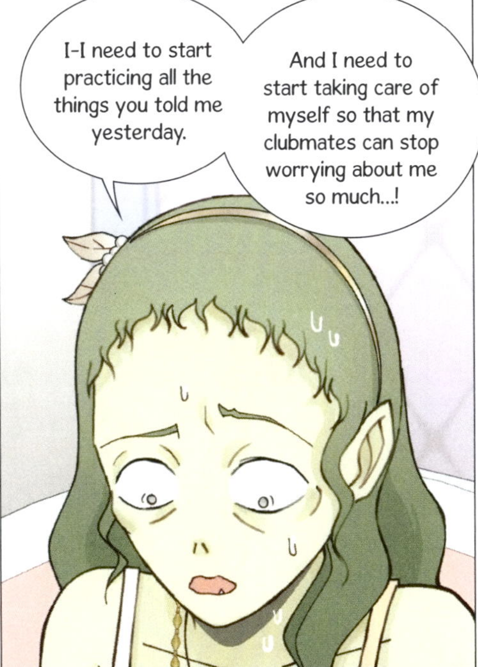

...
...*Sigh*
...You'll never learn to love yourself...
if you can't honestly face your own feelings.
That's a fine goal, Gwendolyn. But...
To be continued!

And now, a brief interlude for...
Maria's Dream
All right, kids! We've read enough of *Little Red Riding Hood* for one night. It's time for bed!
Don't forget the moral of the story, okay? Men are wolves!
Little Red Riding Hood
Yes, Father!

Z Z Z
Goodbye, mother! I'm off to visit members of my fan club!
I don't like these fan visits. Be careful, my darling son!
step
step

Hello! I've come to visit my fans!
knock
knock
Yes! Please come in!
I ♥ BLAINE
My, what big ears you have.
B
I ♥ BLAINE
All the better to hear your interviews and albums with.

And what big hands you have!
All the better to grab your merch with!
And, oh my, what big teeth you have...!
ALL THE BETTER TO **EAT YOU WITH!!**
AAAAAH!!!

SLAM!

Chapter
3

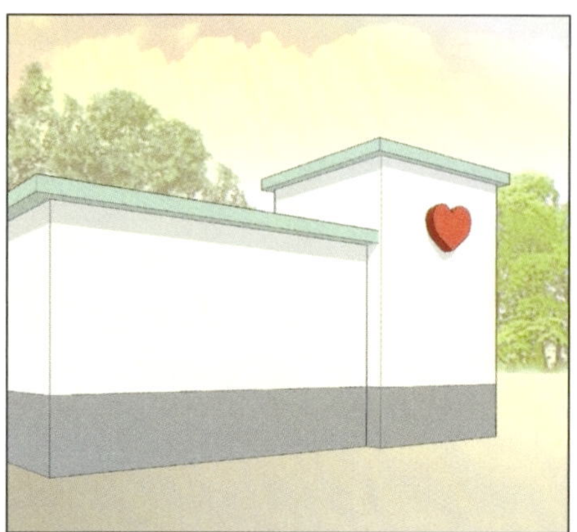

Well, guys, I'm worried about Gwen.

You dragged us all into some cramped closet to tell us that?!
We're supposed to be volunteering at the hospital flower shop right now!
And you know I love flowers!
Yeah, but I had to find a secret place where we could continue our previous conversation privately!

What previous conversation?
Come on, Monika! How could you forget?!
It was when we looked at Gwen's family portrait...

...It's really strange that Gwen doesn't look anything like the rest of her family...

Maybe Gwen **IS** cursed...

I mean, if Gwen is cursed and doesn't know it...
it'll only cause her more confusion and possibly hinder her ability to accept herself.
So who better to look into it than us, the Cursed Princess Club?

Creeeak~
Okay, Syrah, what's our first step?
Wait. Did you guys hear that?!

Well...I was thinking that we don't know anything about Gwen's parents.
I mean, her dad's the king here, but he's **very** secretive. I think something's afoot.
Kind of smells like a foot in here...

Gwen's joining us to volunteer in a little while.
So let's start with some gentle inquiries about her parents.
But be careful. This could be a sensitive topic.

Sounds good. And I agree that we should keep this just between us.
We don't want any rumors about Gwen floating around the Cursed Princess Club.
Saffron's right. This closet gives me the creeps...
Now let's get back to work.

Where's the door?
fumble
Oh jeez, there was a lamp here the whole time.

fwoosh~
wheeze
Oops. Uhh... Guess this was a patient's room
M-maybe he's asleep and didn't hear what we said...

No, I heard everything...
tremble~
...

POOF!
Oh no... Monika, calm down!

AAAHH!!
Good god, what are you trying to do with that pillow, you psychotic hand?!

Uhh, you're still asleep, sir!!
We're all just imaginary monsters in your fever dream!

grow
...Seeee?

...Oh. Okay.
snore
...

Let's get the heck out of here...
Z
Z
Z

Later that afternoon...

step

step

step

I guess we're volunteering at the hospital flower shop today...

This is the first time I'm seeing the Cursed Princess Club since the whole incident with Aurelia.

I have a lot of regrets about it. I wonder how they've been feeling...

Hi, everyone! Sorry I'm late, but I'm here to...

turn

I wish Aurelia could be given another chance to return...

...though I don't know if Prez has ever reconsidered a member's banishment.

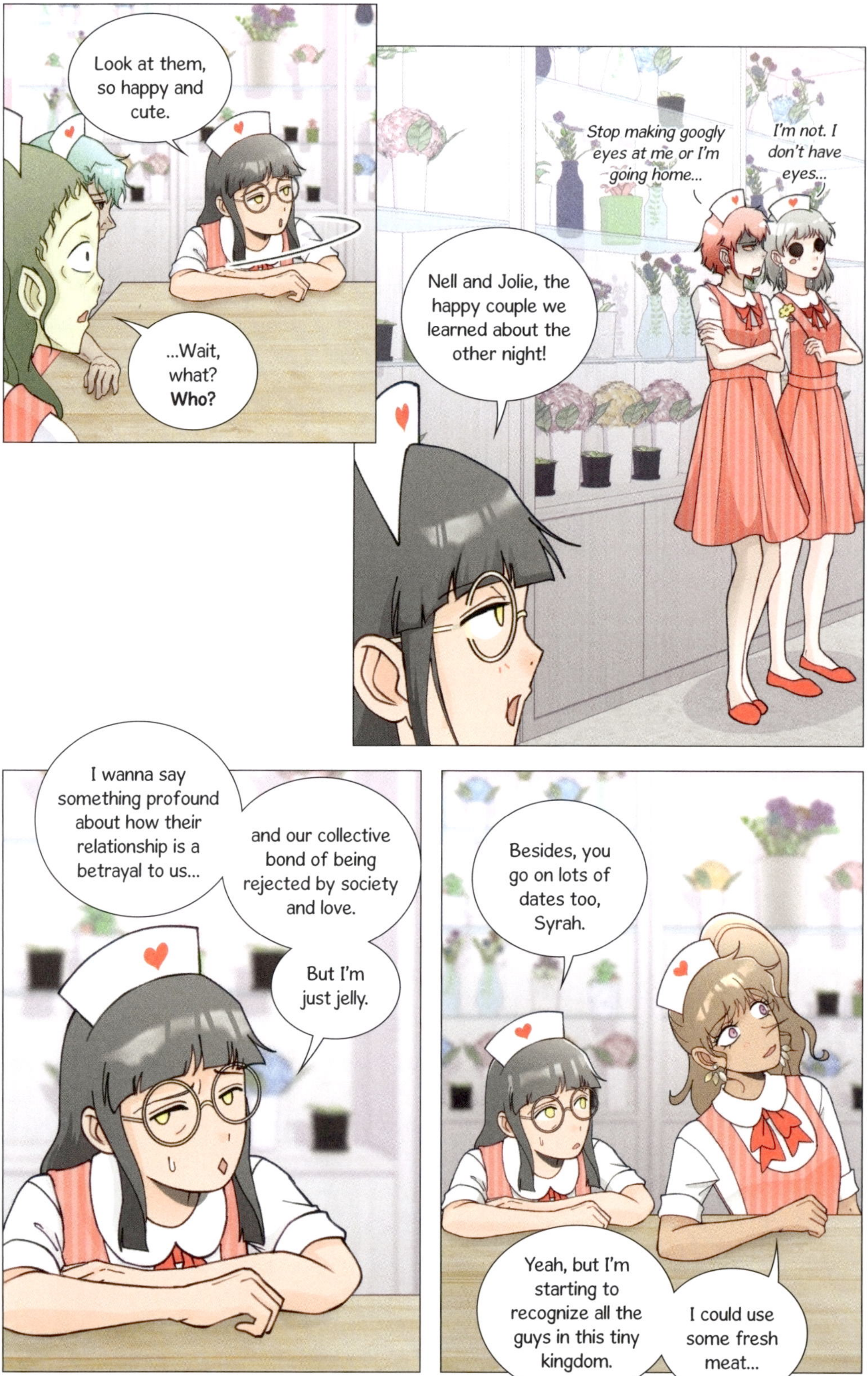

Look at them, so happy and cute.
...Wait, what? **Who?**
Nell and Jolie, the happy couple we learned about the other night!
Stop making googly eyes at me or I'm going home...
I'm not. I don't have eyes...

I wanna say something profound about how their relationship is a betrayal to us...
and our collective bond of being rejected by society and love.
But I'm just jelly.

Besides, you go on lots of dates too, Syrah.
Yeah, but I'm starting to recognize all the guys in this tiny kingdom.
I could use some fresh meat...

Hi! Welcome to the flower shop! How may we help you?
Yeah, can we get flowers delivered up to our dad in room 203?
We love him, but we don't wanna, like, see him or anything...
Oh, I should probably tell Prez that I'm here.

Say, can you point me to the ICU?
Because I **see you** and me having dinner tonight.

So how about a discount on these flowers, hot stuff...?

Oh...No, I'm sorry, we can't do that. We're just volunteers.

Fine! Well, I was lying. I'd never date a dweeb like you!!
Who wears a sweater vest with one glove?! Yuck.
And I'd never date you either!
You look like an uptight chick who bites dudes' heads off on her period.
SLAM

...How did you know that...?!

These flowers better put us in Dad's will, or I'm coming back for a refund!
Aaah–!!
Whack!
stomp
stomp

Um, I can get these!
Thanks, kiddo! Customer service isn't for the faint of heart, is it?

HOW YA BEAN, BUDDY?

Anyhow, let's get you into our production line, Gwen!
Hey, everyone! We got our first order!!

YAAAAY!

Just 'cause this dude's kids are jerks, doesn't mean he shouldn't get some nice flowers.

The petals look a little translucent, but overall these flowers seem pretty well cared for.

They should be good to go with a fresh cut at the stems!

Roger!

snip!

All that's left is to write a heartfelt card on behalf of those brats to their dad.
scribble

Um...on that note...
How's your dad doing, Gwen? He sounds hunky—I mean **healthy**!!
We agreed to find out whether Gwen is cursed or not. The first step is to learn more about her parents...!

Oh, Papa's doing well! We don't get to spend too much time with him, though.
He's really busy, and he leaves town for expeditions a lot.

Expeditions? What does he do on those?

Um...hmm, I don't actually know...
He always tries to tell us about them, but for some reason...
I can't remember what he says...

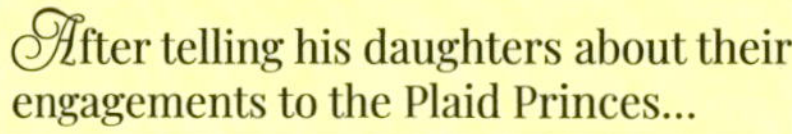

En route to the Plaid Kingdom for Prince Lance's birthday party...

...Now I have to tell you kids about the driftwood that we saw on this latest expedition.

You can learn a lot about your environment by inspecting the knots on driftwood...

and, boy, did this driftwood have a story to tell...

Hey, everyone! Sorry to interrupt!
I just want to say that it's time for me to take off now!
Oh, right— where are you going again, Prez?
Well, as you know, my curse enables me to chat with spiders.
It's mostly spider gossip, but occasionally their network of communication...
can help me locate potential new members for the Cursed Princess Club.
And when I was in the barn a few days ago...
they said they got a new lead on someone!
This person should currently be camping just outside the of Pastel Kingdom.
And guess what...It's a prince!!

YESSS, a new prince!! We've needed another dude for a while now!
Clap!
Fresh meat!!!
And we need a new member, anyhow, since...
...um...since Aurelia is gone...

...Y-yeah. So I'm gonna leave on a solo reconnaissance mission tonight...
...and scope out if they might be a good fit or not.
...Um, as for who should be in charge of the club until I return...
Hmm, let's go with Saffron this time.
What? Me?! This is the day I've always dreamed of!!
The Cursed Princess Club is going to be under my rule, which means I can finally change the name!!
Until Prez comes back...
Everyone, be respectful to Saffron while I'm gone, okay?
I don't want any parties, injuries, or anything out of the ordinary happening—

THUMP-
URGH...!!

AAAGH...!!
Nell...!! Is it happening again?!

What's happening??!! I'll go find a doctor!!!

No...they can't help with this...
Nell's having one of her premonitions of misfortune.
All we can do is make sure she's lying safely on her side, away from any sharp corners or objects...
and hope it subsides as quickly and painlessly as possible.

Premonitions of misfortune...?

That's right...

Nell's family used her for her premonitions and kept her locked below their palace...

until Prez stole her away and formed the Cursed Princess Club...

Yeah, well, I stepped on it, and it really sucked!!
My first act as president of this club is to confiscate all earrings! This ain't happening on my watch!!
Five minutes in and you're already a tyrant.
I...I think it's about to happen...
SOMETIME BEFORE THE NEW MOON WILL PASS...
...A MEMBER OF THIS CLUB SHALL DIE IN A FLASH.
What the...?
Clink

Okay, she's never said **that** before.

B-but it's fine, everyone! Don't forget that Nell's premonitions don't always come true!

Just **mostly**. So let's not panic and—

When I die, just give me a beard at my funeral!!

When I die, tell my dear Benedict that I love him!!

When I die, please—

BLARGAGHH!

No! That's the **opposite** of not panicking!

Okay, okay, I'm gonna cancel my trip to scout that potential new member of the CPC.

So let's just finish volunteering and then go home and relax—

Yeah, and you canceling your trip doesn't make me feel any better!
The potential new member's a man, right?!
Well, if you wanna make me feel better, I need the man! **NOW!!**
I-I can't do that, guys.
Regardless of whether Nell's premonition comes true or not...
...she specifically stated that a member of this club is in danger.
So I can't in good faith recruit a new member and potentially put their life at risk!
Okay! So we just need to figure out who Nell saw die in her premonition.
If it's not some new guy, then Prez is free to go ahead with her mission!
Yeah, that seems easy enough!

Heyyy, Nell... Um, who did you see in your premonition?
Was it a man? Did you see a big hot man, Nell?
I don't know. It's blurry...

Well, **ZOOM AND ENHANCE, NELL!!**

Knock it off and back away from Nell!!
I'm not going, and that settles it!
The new member will have to wait for some other day. And if we miss him, that's too bad!

Okay...
B-but—

Now everyone start heading for the hospital cafeteria!
We're taking a snack break and it's MANDATORY!

step
step
And you **WILL** eat tater tots if I order a plate of them...
We'll **ALL** eat some tots...

Ah, I'm stuffed...

It's funny how a little fried potato can make me feel so much better...

Will that be all for you today, ladies?
I see you're all hospital volunteers, and such pretty ones at that!
May I offer you all some complimentary desserts for your hard work?
We just got some love-themed fortune cookies!

Oh, no thanks.
I think we've had enough fortunes for one day—

What are you saying, Prez?! The only way to combat a bad fortune is to get MORE fortunes!
That's right!! If we just piece together all our fortunes...
we could eventually see **the future**!

That doesn't make any sense...
Haha, I'll bring a plate right away, then.

Okay, guys, I get it.
After hearing Nell's premonition, you're all worried about what might happen.
But I don't want you to be scared into thinking you have no agency over your future!

So I'm making a rule! Before we open our fortune cookies...
we each have to state one action we can take to tackle a current fear or regret in our lives!
Sigh Fine...

Okay, Syrah, why don't you go first.
An action I can take to better live life without regret?

Well, there IS this one thing I've always wanted to try where you line up a bunch of guys and—
All right!! Who's next?!

Abbi!! How about you?
M-me...?

Well...I mean, this whole thing does make me anxious to finally confess my feelings to my crush, Bobby...

That's right, Abbi has had a crush on this boy for a while...
...and even wanted to make a potion to try to reverse her curse for a day...
...in order to dance with him at her prom.

I don't want to regret not telling him how special he is to me...
But part of me knows it's a terrible idea...
because there's no way he'll return my feelings. And it'll hurt.

Abbi...

Um...I can't say whether you should or not. But...
it made me remember when I overheard what Frederick said about me and how it really hurt.
Yeah. I still wanna hit him...

But...if I'd never had that awful feeling...
I never would have run into the forest and met you guys.
And that's one of the best things that's ever happened in my life.

Things are also better now with Frederick, thanks to all of you.
We're friends now, and...
it's nice...

Thanks, Gwen.
I guess good things can still happen even if they don't go the way you want them to.
Wait...If I'm thankful for all the things that led me to become a part of the Cursed Princess Club...
...then does that mean...
...I should also be thankful for the way I look...?

Also, whatever. If Bobby turns me down...
I always have Prez as my backup crush.
Your—
huh...?!

Yeah, who doesn't? It's Prez's harem, and we're all living in it.
Hey!! Don't call this my harem!!
H-here are your fortune cookies...

And thank you, Abbi, but...you're a little young for me.
shrug
Geez, lady, how old do you want 'em?

Anyway, it's your turn, Prez.
Do you have any romantic regrets or fears you've been stuck on?
...I never said these were supposed to be romantic...

Are you still hung up on those two guys from your past?
Huh??!! What are you talking about?!

My feelings for Asa were always just of deep admiration.

He's still who I strive to be, and I'll never forget everything he did for me.

And Prince Whitney?! Of course I'm not hung up on him!

He was a despicable monster...

CRACK!
Hmpf...
It's not too late to reach out and forgive.

...?
It's what's inside the book that matters.

Ah! My fortune!!
drop!
Oh—I can get that...

There it is...
SWOOP

Your love life looks bleak and barren

Come on, do they have to word it like that?!

Hmm, I don't think a little switcheroo would hurt anybody...

Here you go, Abbi.
Thanks, Prez!

"You will reunite with a boy from your past!"
Ooh!! I don't know who this fortune is referring to, but I'm excited now!

That's great, Abbi!

pant
pant
pant
drag-
groan
Ughhh, this carriage is even harder to pull...
than if I were to just carry Laverne on my back.

I don't even know where I am anymore.
I think we're somewhere near the border of the Pastel Kingdom.
I'm so exhausted and hungry.

Would you like to take a rest here?
Gasp!

Wh-who's there?! Who are you?!
I didn't mean to startle you...
I'm just a fellow traveler.

My name's Whitney...
of the Monochrome Kingdom.

Chapter
4

Good evening, Father!
step
step
Oh, hey, boys.
CHESS YOU CAN!
How was your visit with the Pastel Princesses today?

We had a lovely time!
We each got to take the princesses somewhere they wanted to go.
And they both accepted our invitations to the big gala!

Pastel Plaza Jewelers
Is there a particular reason you wanted to go jewelry shopping, Maria?
Um, well...you said your mom likes charm bracelets, right?
Which one of these do you think she would like better?

Oh...! Why, that's incredibly thoughtful of you, Maria...
especially considering you haven't even met Mother yet!
I don't approve of any of this arranged marriage nonsense.
I guess that means she never told Blaine about our chat at Lance's party...
I wonder why. Is she testing me?
U-um, yeah! I just figured that...
some messages are best conveyed with a little gift!
I actually couldn't agree more.
You see, while you were browsing gifts for Mother...
...I got you a small trinket too...
in celebration of your increased freedom outside your palace walls!
Gasp
Blaine...!

Oh my gosh, it's lovely!!

Wait, what is this attached to it...?

Bippity Bop

ADMIT ONE

Will you attend the gala with me, Maria?

Yes, Blaine! I'd love to!!

PLAID KINGDOM
FENCING ACADEMY
And Suzanna Winchester wins the bout fifteen to four!!
Yaaaay, Suzie!!
Cheer~!!
WIN CHES TER
What is **SHE** doing here...?!!
The only guy I want to notice me is finally watching...
stomp stomp
...but only **AFTER** he got engaged to this nincompoop!
Did you just come here to heckle me with Prince Lance?!!
Chomp
Chomp
No, silly, we're here to cheer you on!

Cheer me on?...Is she really so stupid that she thinks we're actually friends?

Chomp
Chomp
So you wanna come over and spar sometime?!
...I-I don't know. My schedule's really busy...
WIN CHES TER

Now that I can leave my palace, I can really add to my weapons collection, and—
Chomp
Chomp
WIN CHES TER

chew-
...What ith thith...?
WIN CHES

bleh~
...?
YES, I'll go to the gala with you, Lance!!!
A-awesome...
Splat
Never mind!! I'm coming over and beating you to a pulp in your own home!!!

So where's Frederick? I wanna tell him he really missed out today.
Oh, he's not here.
He left earlier this afternoon for the Pastel Palace with Laverne.
CHESS

Th-this afternoon...?!
...But it's pretty late now...Where is he?!

Somewhere just outside the border of the Pastel Kingdom...

I've run into a giant, terrifying-looking man...

...who could definitely kill me with one hit...
Hey...

...And yet he's just been really nice and shared his dinner with us!
shake
Do you or your pet llama want seconds?

I also just boiled some hot water for tea, if you'd like some.
Do you prefer chamomile or ginger root?

I've never met someone so intimidatingly hospitable...

Umm...I think we're both good, thank you.
Sorry about Laverne, by the way...
whimper-
She usually loves every guy she meets, but I've never seen her so scared...

Oh. No, that's understandable.
It's one of the many side effects that emerged once I started looking like this.
I now seem to have an aura that frightens most animals around me.

Oh yeah, um, that's...an **interesting** face tattoo.
Uh... wh-why'd you get that?

Face tattoo...?
Oh, you mean these tiger stripes...
And why did I get them...?
Um, I guess you could say I got them because I needed a humbling reminder of a very important life lesson...

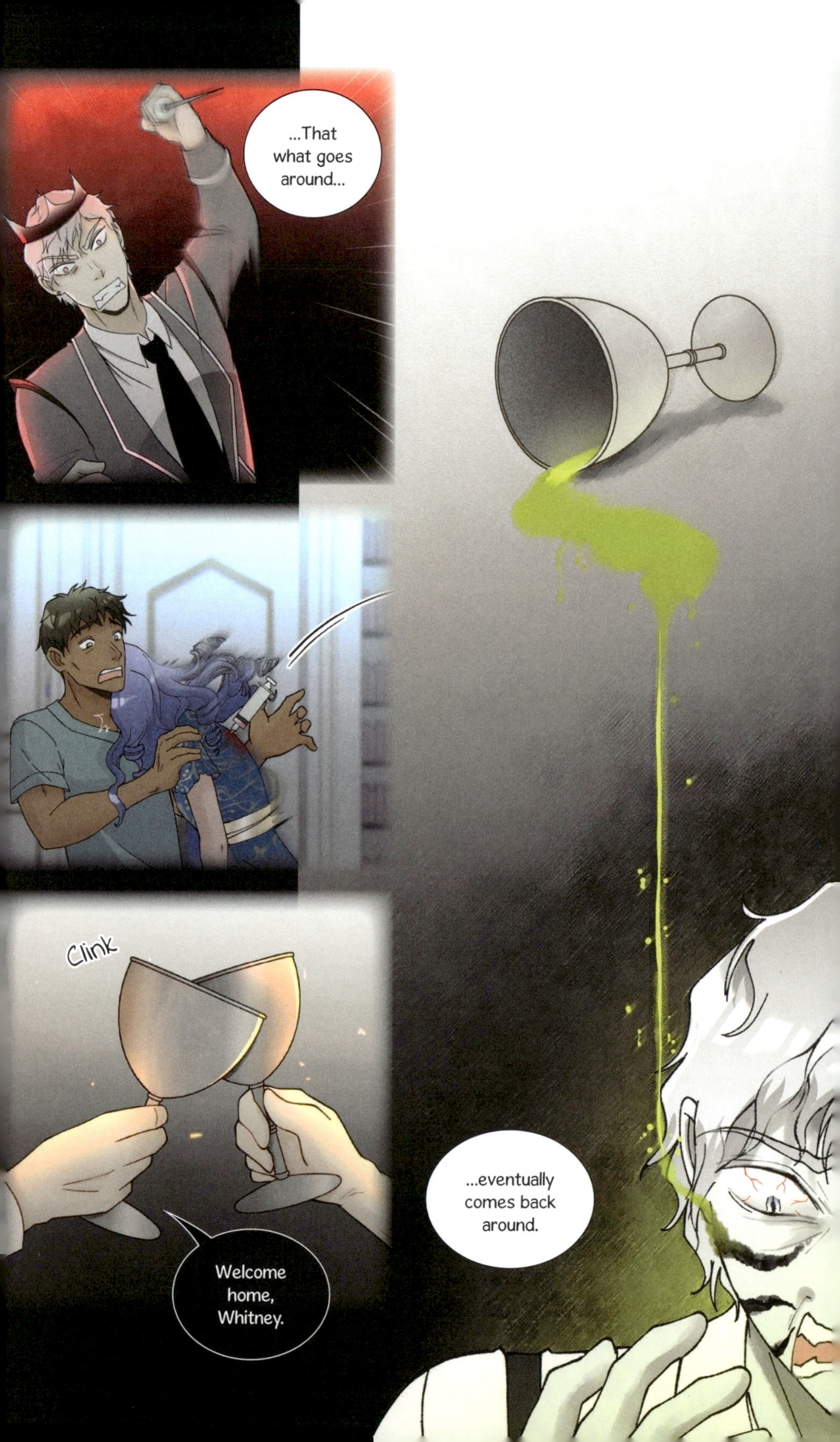
...That what goes around...
Clink
Welcome home, Whitney.
...eventually comes back around.

If he needed a reminder of that lesson so badly...
I feel like a tattoo of the quote would have been a better choice. But whatever...
I-I'm sorry, I don't think I understand...

I wouldn't want to subject a kid to such a grueling tale right now.
But to put it lightly...

...I was a really bad person...

I was a person who spiraled out of control in pursuit of getting everything I thought I was entitled to.

It got to a point where I didn't care if it ruined people's lives...
...or if it almost cost me my own.

I-I don't think I understand much about what you're saying...
but I can definitely relate to you about your cutthroat family.

Really? Wow, it's comforting to meet another person who's gone through something like this.
Yeah...it is, actually...

The endless competitions and comparisons...
nod

The violent, gladiator-style fights to win Father's affection each week...
...Th-the what...?

...The contests to see which son could most effectively torture political prisoners...
...Oh...Oh god...

Oh! Did you have to recite those daily Machiavellian chants too?
N-nope! Can't say I did...!

So allow me to pass along some wise words I heard.

They're also coincidentally the same words I wish I could tell my father when he had me and my siblings see who could torture prisoners better.

Pain is not a competition.

The painful emotions you feel are valid, Frederick.
But you do get to choose when you're ready to heal from them and change your story.

This is the weirdest dude I've ever met...
Um...So what exactly are you doing out here in the middle of nowhere?

I've been traveling by foot for a few years now...
making amends to people I've hurt with my past actions.
My last stop is to find a person who now lives somewhere in the Pastel Kingdom...
though I'm not sure where to find them or if they'll be willing to see me.

And may I ask why you are traveling?
M-me?! N-no reason, really!! I'm just out for a stroll...!

Why did you get so sweaty and weird just now...?
Sorry, that's another consequence of this curs— I mean these tiger stripes...
I'm really keen at sensing fear and panic in others.
So...what is it? Are you seeing a girl or something?
Sh-she's a friend! I **think**...! I-I mean, I don't even know why I'm here!
Y-you know, actually, I feel really refreshed after that stew!
So I think we're just gonna head back home now!!
Let's go, Laverne!
bleeeat?!
Whoa, whoa, wait!
It's really late out now, and there are coyotes around these parts.

It would be safer for you and your llama to call it a night for now...
...and decide where you'd like to go in the morning.
Would you like to camp out here? I have a tent.

How would us all sleeping in that flimsy tent protect us from coyotes, though?

Oh, the tent's for you two. I just bring it in case I meet travelers who need one.
I sleep in the grass. And **I'm** the protection.
Just like your llama, coyotes seem to want to stay far away from where I am.

shrug
Um...well, okay.
I guess we'll take you up on your offer.

One hour later...
Yep, that's one weird dude...
stare

chirp
chirp

blink
Uhh...it's so sunny...
I feel something really warm and fluffy and...

Z
Z
Z
drool
...HEAVY!
Where am I...?!!

Oh...right...
I camped out overnight in the middle of nowhere with this eccentric guy.
Oh! Good morning, Frederick.
Would you like some deer meat?
Crackle

Chomp
Mmm! Where'd you get such fresh-tasting meat around here?!
chew
Uhh... Where'd I get it?

Pfffft!
I guess from, like, right there...?

So, Frederick, now that you've slept on it...
have you decided where you want to go today?
Are you gonna visit your, uh, friend?
Or head back home?

Huh?!...
Um, n-no.
I haven't
decided...
...What **am** I doing...?!
Everything was so
clear yesterday when
I left, but...that seems
like so long ago.
Blaine and Lance
have probably long
since visited the
princesses and
returned home...
So...am I too
late? What was
the point of even
going?
Um, I-I think
I'm just gonna
go home.
My thoughts
are all foggy
and messy right
now...
a-and I have
no clue what
I'm even doing
anymore...
Oh...well, I
can help with
that if you
want.
I can show
you one of
the things I
learned...
from the people
who took me in
after I left my
kingdom.
What...?
Really?
You know...
you keep saying
you were this
awful person or
whatever...
...but you turned
your life around
after meeting
these amazing
people.
Who are
they?

Hmm, I guess I would describe them as...
beings that I couldn't even believe existed when I was younger...

Beings that he couldn't even believe existed when he was younger?
They sound mythical or even magical...

When I finally realized how toxic my life was...
I kept trying to change, but I found it really difficult a lot of the time.
I felt like my mind was being bombarded every second by deeply terrible thoughts and urges...
that would fill my head up and make me forget everything I was trying to do.

I carried so many harrowing and shameful memories...
that my brain can't seem to let me forget, no matter how hard I try...
Once again, even though he seems so odd, I can really relate to what he says sometimes...

All the horrible things I used to think...
all the regretful things I've done...

...all the torturing of others in the torture dungeon, all the in the dungeon, all the—
NOPE, I take it back again...!
UGH, okay, okay! I get it!! Jeez!

Anyway, I learned that those memories aren't trying to hurt us.
But they can get a little out of control and fill our heads up with thoughts that aren't useful to us anymore.

So if you can clear some of that clutter away...
you can sometimes start to see what's really in front of you in a different light.
H-how would I even do that?

By sitting and making some room.
...Would you like to try?

It may not be right for everyone...
and it will be hard at first...
but the more you do it, the easier it will get.
For starters, just close your eyes and sit quietly.
...?
close
...Uh... okay.

...Hmm?

SER LOSER

LOSER LOSER

FAILURE FAILURE FAILURE

FAILURE FAIL E FAILURE

LOSER FAILURE ER

SER FAILURE LOSE LURE LOS

Hmm...Do it just once more, if you can.
But this time try to listen for where the voice is coming from.
And if you do meet the source...be kind.

Meet the source...?! What is he talking about?
Uh...sure, just once more.

Sigh...
close

SER LOSER
R LOSER L
SER LOSER

LOSER LOSER LOSER
LOSER LOSER LOSER
FAILURE FAILURE FAILURE
LOSER FAILURE LOSER FAILURE
FAILURE FAILURE FAILURE

Wait...

THAT'S the source of the mean voice that's always playing in my head?

Isn't that me when I was at boarding school?

LOSER LOSER LOSER
FAILURE FAILURE FAILURE

And isn't that the trunk that I was locked in by those bullies?

Um... hey.
Wh-why are you sitting in there?

What d'you mean? I can't get out.
Not that I care, though. I'd rather be in here, anyway.

You...can't get out of that...?
It doesn't even cover your knees, though...
Uhh...okay, well, I can pull you up...

...
lift
Sooo, what do you wanna do now?
You gonna go build forts with books and build model ships like you used to?

No, that's for losers, you **stupid loser**!
We don't do those things anymore because people make fun of us for it! How could you forget that?!
Ohhh boy...
And **first** of all...

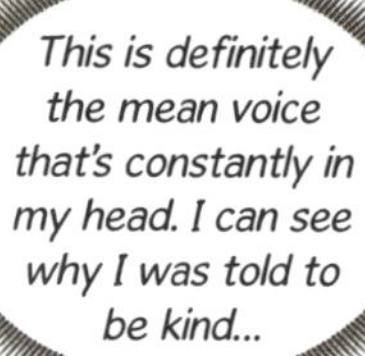
This is definitely the mean voice that's constantly in my head. I can see why I was told to be kind...
...but these negative words don't seem to carry the same weight now that I know they're coming from a small child...

There's no time for books and hobbies anyway!
We have to catch up to Blaine and Lance!
Um...d-do we really, though?

Yes, we do!!
They always laugh at us and look down on us for being the family failure!
They don't even wanna be associated with us!

I-I **did** think that, but...I kinda feel like they do care, and I just didn't notice.
Yeah, they're busy a lot of the time and they can be pretty self-absorbed, but...
sometimes they look out for us too.

...Fine, well, the Blaine Fan Club is still a pile of doo-doo.

Can't disagree with you there, buddy.

Anyway, I hate even being near the Pastel Kingdom, so I'm gonna climb back in here.
What?! NO!! Don't go back in there, you little—!
climb
Why do you hate the Pastel Kingdom so much?

Because something weird or terrifying always happens at that stupid place...
and it's usually when Gwen's around!!
Hey!! Gwen's actually...n-not so bad...
grab
Yeah, not so bad at scaring the crap out of you!

Okay...I-I guess I misunderstood some things about her at first.
Actually, there're still some things I don't understand...
A-and there are definitely things that are...**different** about her
But, um...
...there's also...
...something that's...
...really special.

Yeah, well, she's definitely no Angel of Fortune!!
She can't lift us up or protect us from anyone out there—
Maybe we don't **need** someone to protect us, huh?!
Maybe I can figure out how to protect myself! A-and Gwen too!
Wait, why would you even bother protecting Gwen?
BECAUSE I DON'T LIKE IT WHEN PEOPLE SAY MEAN THINGS ABOUT THE GIRL I LIKE!
...
open
...!!

Uh, hey...
How did it go?
You realize
anything?
Y-yeah. I
realized...

Thank you for
everything you've
done for me!!
The next time I
see you again, I
promise I'll repay
you!
dash
Wait! I don't
care about
that, but you
need to know
that...
one session of
this isn't enough
to change your
mindset forever!!
Your willpower...

...I realized that
I need to see
Gwen! **NOW!!**
stand

...will run
out...

Laverne, it's
time to get up!
And you're lying
on my book—
OW! Don't
slap my hand
away!

SCREECH_!!
Pant
Must...
drag~
...get...
Groooan
...to the Pastel Palace...
SCREEECH!
...!!
step
step
step
Uh, hey again. I'm...headed this way too...
Uhh. D-didn't expect to run into you so quickly again...
I-I'll pay you back the **next** next time...
Again, I really don't care about that.
But do you need some help fixing your cart? I don't think it was assembled very well...
N-no, it's fine! Really!! You've helped me enough!
And Laverne's getting really impatient, so I can't stop until we reach our destination—
Um, are you sure? Because...
trot
trot
HEY...!!
splat!
...I think she just walked away.
Bleeeaaat—! (Translation: I'm finding a bar, and I'll meet you there.)
To be continued!

Frederick's Dream

I guess Gwen liked this book I lent her.

I'm kind of glad...

I know it's just a silly children's fairy tale, but...

...it still means a lot to me for some reason.

yawn~

Maybe part of me still wishes it could come true or something.

A man is stuck in a hole and can't climb out, no matter how much he tries.
And the rest of the village looks down on him.
One day, an Angel of Fortune appears above him and pulls him out with ease...
Wait, that's me in the hole...
I can't lift you any further, though.
You'll have to pull yourself up from here...
Gwen is my Angel of Fortune...?
What she said sounds a little different from the book, though.

With her by his side, the man became admired and respected by everyone in the village.
He gained love and courage he never knew he could have.
And when the time came, he prepared to battle the giant serpent.
H-huh?! The serpent...
The serpent is—

AAAH!!

Wait... there was something else in that dream...

I can't remember anymore.

Chapter 5

While Frederick inched his way closer to the Pastel Palace...
Almost... there...
huff

Leopold began his third day of painting Gwen's portrait.

Where is he...?
Where is that pink glittery gremlin going to pop out from next...?!

Ever since he made that declaration against me...

...he keeps popping up out of nowhere...

...and it's always whenever I'm trying to get closer to Gwendolyn!!

But then why...

why do these hands keep drawing him every time he appears?!

I've ruined stacks of paper and canvas with his maniacally cherubic features!

Last night...

His visage has even started to terrorize me outside of work...

B-B-Bart, bring me a snack to calm my nerves! I've had a long day of it!

Here, my lord...

BEGONE, PINK DEMON!!!

Oh my, I mixed up your snack with your niece's cotton candy.

But what's gotten into you lately, my lord?

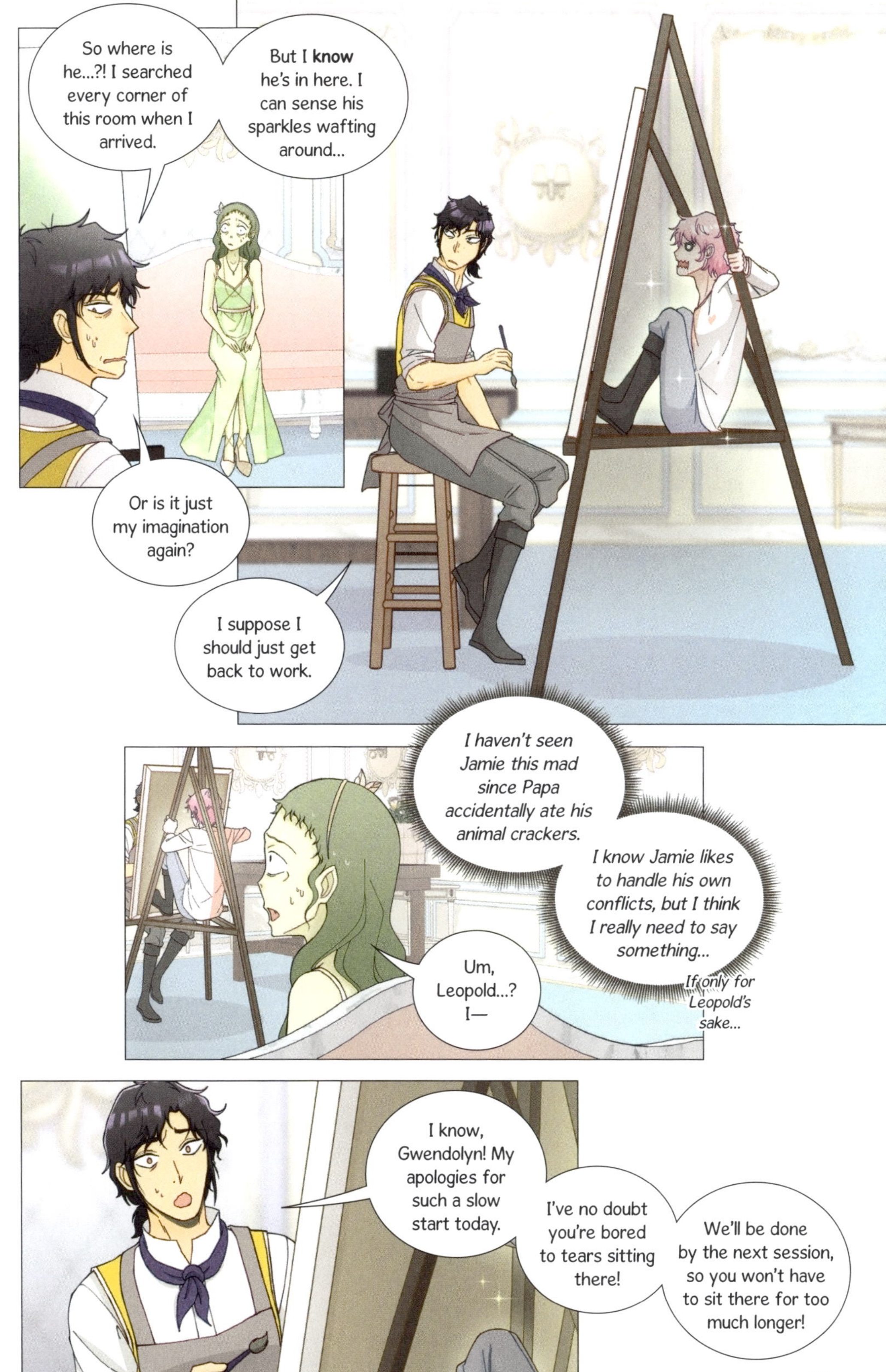
So where is he...?! I searched every corner of this room when I arrived.
But I **know** he's in here. I can sense his sparkles wafting around...
Or is it just my imagination again?
I suppose I should just get back to work.
I haven't seen Jamie this mad since Papa accidentally ate his animal crackers.
I know Jamie likes to handle his own conflicts, but I think I really need to say something...
If only for Leopold's sake...
Um, Leopold...? I—
I know, Gwendolyn! My apologies for such a slow start today.
I've no doubt you're bored to tears sitting there!
We'll be done by the next session, so you won't have to sit there for too much longer!

O-oh, I don't mind at all! But, um—

point

Ah! Gwendolyn, it's important at this stage...

that you don't make any movements while I capture these minute details.

To keep some portrait subjects from feeling too restless...

I'll usually ask them questions to pass the time, if that is all right with you.

So, Gwendolyn...
Let's see what
I can ask you...
What's your
favorite
season?
Hmm, I guess
right about now,
when all the leaves
change orange for
autumn.

And what's
your favorite
hobby?
To make things
and give them to
people.

That's a lovely
hobby.
rustle
Um...I apologize if
this next question
is too personal,
but...
it's something
I've been
wanting to ask
you for a while.

Gwendolyn...
do you have
romantic feelings
for Prince
Frederick?

...!

Please be honest with your feelings, Gwendolyn...
If not out loud, at least to yourself...

D-do I... **what...?!**

Frederick...
One of the first things I learned about him was how he feels about me...
After that, I didn't want to face him again, but I had to.
For the sake of preserving my sisters' engagements...
I told him that we didn't have to be engaged. We could just be friends.
And it's actually been going well. We've gotten to talk more...
and have even discovered some things we have in common.
I really like when we get to spend time together now...
And everything's been really great between our families too...
So...after all that...
...do I have feelings for Frederick?

No.
I won't ever allow that to happen.

Wait, what am I doing?!

This is exactly when I need to keep an eye on Leopold...

...before he makes a move!!!

peek

Sigh

I guess I got the answer I was looking for...

Gwendolyn...you asked me for advice on how to love yourself.
But...no one can help you if you won't even allow yourself to—
...
WHACK!
AAAHH! PINK DEMON!!!!
whoosh—

Uh-oh...

Gasp
The painting!!

NOOOOOO!!!

Whew! Nice teamwork!

There's nothing nice about what you almost did!!
I've painted in some stressful environments before, but this takes the cake!!
Please! Stop terrorizing me and just let me finish my job!!!

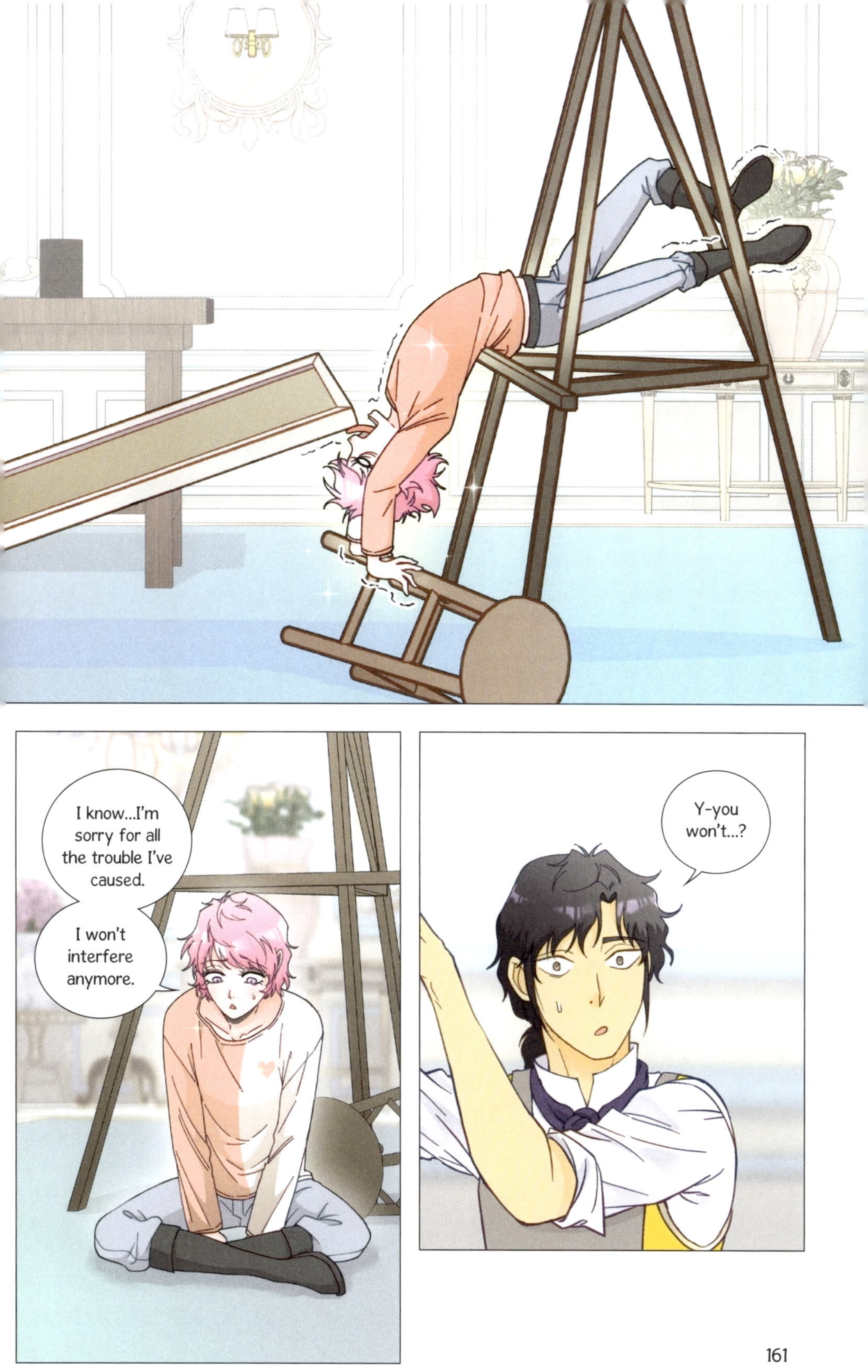

I know...I'm sorry for all the trouble I've caused.
I won't interfere anymore.

Y-you won't...?

I did it because I worry about Gwennie...
and I care about her happiness.
But...it's pretty clear to me now that you do too.

That's why he kept butting in?
Gwennie, I need to apologize to you too...
step
step

Papa's not the only one that's too protective in this family.
But I need to have more faith that you'll do what's best for you.
Thanks, Jamie...

Huh...from this perspective...
perhaps he's not so hideous after all...
sketch
sketch

What?!
How am I sketching again?!

Well...once more couldn't hurt...

scrape
scrape

Is someone at the door?
Come in...!

Hello?
scrape
scrape

pant
pant

huff
I'm almost to the Pastel Palace...
...It's just up this last hill!

And when I get there...I'm going to find Gwen...
a-and ask her to go to the gala with me!!

I mean...if she wants to...

...and if she's not going with someone else already...

It's okay. I don't need to worry about those thoughts right now!

I realized this thanks to that Whitney guy and his meditation thing.

shake

It also helped me realize something else really important.

I think I've been reading that fairy tale wrong this whole time.

Gwen **is** my Angel of Fortune.

I can't lift you up any further.

You'll have to pull yourself up from here...

She reached out to lift me up from the hole I've been stuck in for so long...

...both in real life and in my dream.

But just like she said...

she could only do so much.

I'm the one who ultimately had to pull myself out.

I thought the angel was supposed to lift me up, protect me, and give me courage...
...but it's the other way around.
I want to lift myself up and have courage so that I can protect **her**...!
It all seems so clear now!
pant
pant

I-I'm sorry for parking there!! I'm kind of in a hurry!
dash
thunk

Shoot, I forgot something important...

I'll definitely be needing this...

step
step
If the fairy tale is real, though...
...that means I have to battle the serpent now and protect Gwen!

And that means the serpent must be...

FWOOSH!
GET AWAY FROM HER!!!

...

Sheesh, okay. Sorry...I won't touch Laverne again.
Who knew you'd get so possessive after two road trips with her?

...we spotted Laverne walking out of a bar and grill, so we picked her up.

Laverne, do you know where Frederick is?

Can you lead us to him?!

nod

She has several barrels around her neck...

"Mojito"? "Virgin Bloody Mary"?

How did you buy these?

So we followed her lead...

scrape
scrape
...and she led us to the Pastel Palace for an impromptu cocktail party!
creak-
Uhh...Good afternoon. Is Frederick here?

Um, speaking of cocktails, would you like one, Frederick? Laverne brought a nonalcoholic kind too.
Here's a virgin Bloody Mary... which I think is maybe just tomato juice...
...!
step step

G-Gwen!!!

I'm finally here in front of her...!
I-I feel...
really nervous.

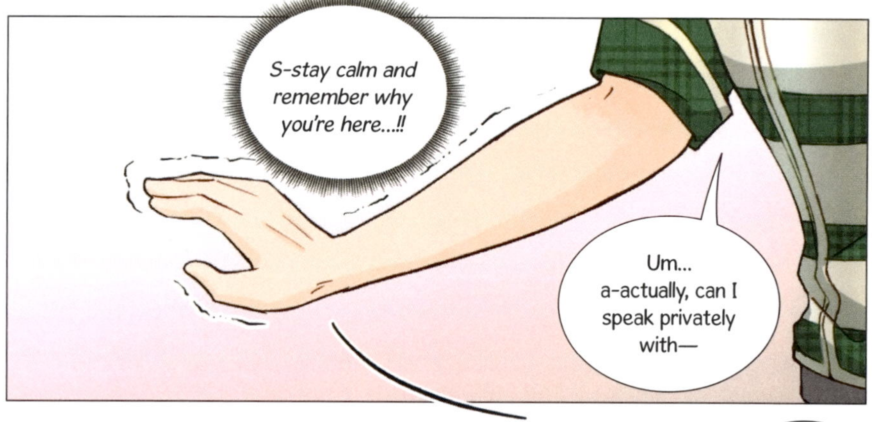
S-stay calm and remember why you're here...!!
Um... a-actually, can I speak privately with—

With the gentlemen, outside in the hall? I was just thinking the same thing, Frederick!
pat

Excuse us for a moment, ladies.
Huh??!!
step
step
step

shove
Hey!! Why did you drag me out into the hall?
I was in the middle of talking with Gwen!

That's great, but you owe an explanation to your big brothers first!

...Wait, why are you guys here?

I dunno. **You're** the one who said for the gentlemen to gather in the hall.
Um, I live here.
Y-yes, Jamie, I know...
Well... okay, fine.

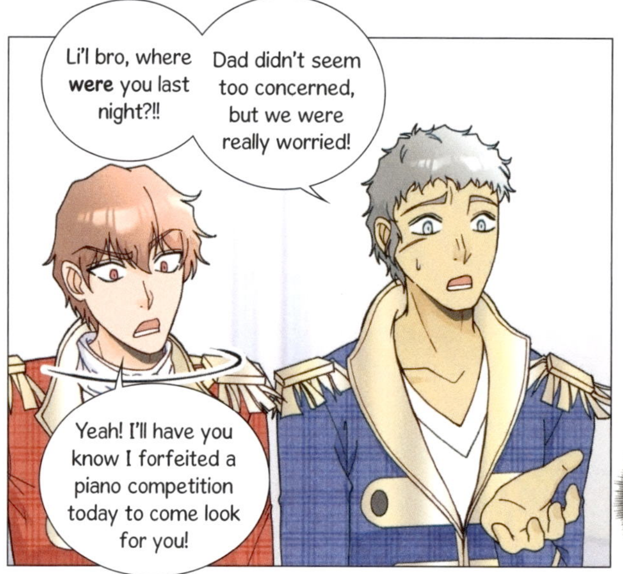
Li'l bro, where **were** you last night?!!
Dad didn't seem too concerned, but we were really worried!
Yeah! I'll have you know I forfeited a piano competition today to come look for you!

What? Blaine forfeited something... for me?!
...But those competitions mean everything to him.

I-I'm really sorry. It's a long story, but I'm fine!
I was traveling here, and it got really late...
but I met this guy on the roadside who let me camp with him.

sob
You slept with a guy you met on the side of the road?
We wanted you to become a man but with more self-respect than that!
DO YOU GUYS ACTUALLY CARE?!

Well, I'm glad you're safe. But we gotta tell Father to stop making you travel with Laverne.
You smell horrible once again, but this time you reek like a cat in a campfire.
...A cat?
You do look pretty tattered.
Why don't we chug our drinks and get you home?
Huh?!! NO! I can't!! I came here to talk to Gwen!
I-I have a **mission** I need to fulfill!
I pulled myself out of the hole and ran here...
a-and I'm supposed to find Gwen and protect her from Leopold the serpent, and—
HEY!!! I'm not a serpent!!
WHACK!
How **dare** you call me that, you mean little worm!
OW!!

Wait...w-was I just getting too overimaginative again...?
Is the fairy tale not real after all?!
...And does that mean Leopold isn't the serpent...
and I don't have to battle him?!
Huh? **Battle** him?! Why?
Ummm... t-to fight for Gwen...
a-and to ask her to the gala...
Oh my god... Frederick!!! You **DID** become a man overnight!!
I never thought I'd hear him say those words!!
Yeeeah, now that I say it in front of other people...
it sounds completely ridiculous.

You hear that, Leopold?!
You Argyle guys are done pulling one over on us!!
step
step

Yeah!! Frederick's challenging you to a duel!
WHAT?! A **DUEL**?!
I never said that!!!

Don't worry, li'l bro! Duels are awesome!
Like the one at my birthday party—that was fun, right?
NOT TO PARTICIPATE IN!!!

sit
I'm not dueling this imbecile.
I'm just here to make art, yet I keep getting interrupted by buffoons.

Do you have romantic feelings for Prince Frederick?

No.

I won't ever allow that to happen.

And though she couldn't say it herself...

...it was crystal clear to me who her heart had already chosen...

...which makes this all the more infuriating.

—!!
Hey, Leopold? Why do you have a sketchbook full of drawings of Jamie?
Weren't you commissioned to paint Gwen?
chomp
AAH! GIVE THAT BACK!!
snatch!
And it's not a sketchbook!
It's a nightmare journal...
I swear, you brothers are all so AGGRAVATING!
You know what? If it's a serpent you seek so badly...
then **fine**. I'm happy to act the part.
Frederick, I accept your duel.
If you defeat me...
then you shall ask Gwendolyn to the gala and get it over with.

But if I win...
you tell her you'll never see her again and stop wasting everyone's time.
Do we have a deal?
Wh-what...?! Why would I agree to **that**?
Yeah, state your own demands, Frederick!!
We got your back, buddy!!
SLAP!
OOF—
...
N-no!
I wasn't shaking your hand! I was just holding it!!
shake

If you're saying you'd like to forfeit, that's fine.
Then you can tell Gwendolyn you won't ever see her again.
I'm sure she won't be too saddened to say goodbye to someone who showed so little conviction anyhow.

And as for the gala...

I'm sure she'll find someone else to go with...

You have a ticket to the gala??!!! B-but... how?!
I'm on the committee for it! Only a few special vendors have access to them at this point, and **you're** not one of them!
The position of the gala's official painter was awarded to my personal portrait artist...
after my rousing recommendation of him!

At Lance's birthday party.
Go eat paint, Leopold. I quit!!
Oh. Uhh, turns out he decided on a... sudden career change...
So they gave me the gig instead.

What?! I lost Pierre?!!
Frederick! Fight this man immediately!! For Pierre's sake!
You can do it! We have faith in you, li'l bro!!!

HUH?! NO WAY! I DON'T HAVE FAITH IN MYSELF!
Look at his eyes—he's gonna kill me!!
Do you forfeit or not, Frederick...?!

N-no!! But...

How did I get into this mess?! I can't say goodbye to Gwen forever!
I know I said I'd be able to figure out how to protect myself and her, but...
...honestly, I don't know how to do any of that yet! There's no way I can win!

I-I'll agree, but only if we compete in something other than a physical duel!
Please, anything at all...!

...Fine.

Oh thank God...
That was a good call, Frederick...
Yeah. He was definitely gonna murder you.

I...obviously choose painting, then.

Crap. Right...art prodigy.
...
Oooh, this is way worse now...

Chapter 6

Sooo...what exactly is going on now?

Uhhh, i-it's just some entertainment to go with our drinks!

I can't tell them what really went on in the hallway...

Ahem...thank you for your patience, ladies and gentlemen.
Preparations have been finalized, and we are now ready to commence...
tug
...the art duel between Prince Frederick of the Plaid Kingdom and Lord Leopold of the Argyle Kingdom!

smooch-

...the immaculate Laverne!

...I mean, that just seemed fair...
shrug

To be clear, I'm well aware that your brothers are trying to give you an advantage. But it's fine by me...
because there's still no way you will win, Frederick.
So I'm perfectly delighted to paint your Rubenesque dog over there.

...Rubenesque?!
...Dog?!

Bleeeeat! (Translation: Avenge meee–!)
I wouldn't get your hopes up, Laverne.

All right, gentlemen. You have thirty minutes.
On your mark...
get set...
...paint!!

Okay...That's... that could be a foot. Maybe...
SWOOSH~
...
peek
I'M NOT A PRODIGY! I'M A LOSER!!!
This isn't a contest—it's utterly hopeless! What's the point in even trying?!

Good luck!

...!

Right...**She's** the reason I'm trying...
...Come to think of it, she kind of always makes me **want** to try...

Okay! This isn't over!! Don't lose sight of what you're trying to do!
FREDERICK'S WILLPOWER METER
You have your willpower, and that's all you need!!!

Twenty-nine minutes later...
FREDERICK'S WILLPOWER METER
Nope, willpower is NOT all you need...
You need painting skills too!

Frederick sure is taking this art contest seriously. Is he okay?

I don't know...
This entire time, I've just been staring at Blaine's glass I offered to hold while he officiates the match.
I-if I just take a sip...it'll be like a **kiss**...the kiss we haven't had yet!

Sigh How is this entertainment again?
They're just standing and painting really quietly!

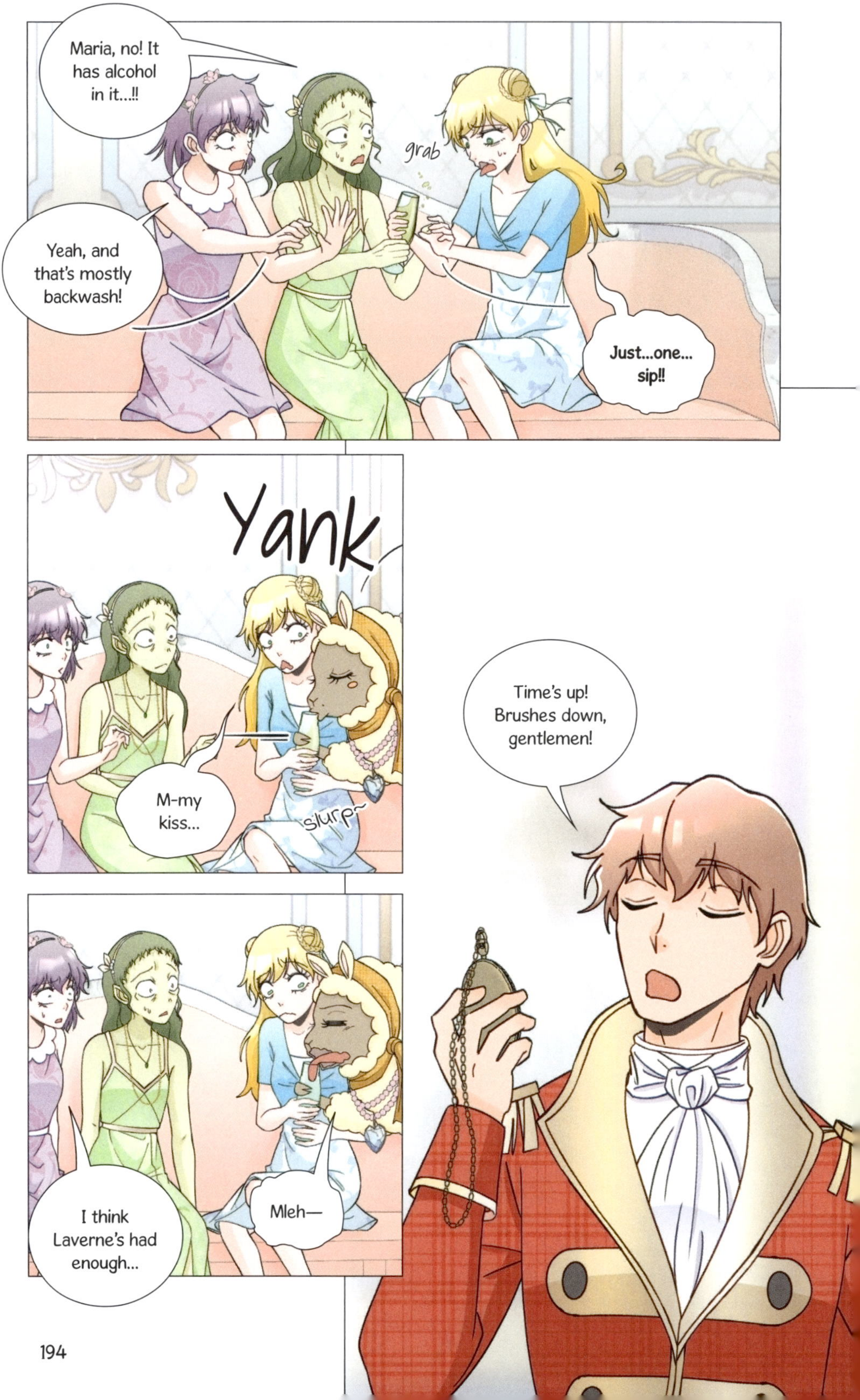

Yank
M-my kiss...
slurp~
Time's up! Brushes down, gentlemen!
I think Laverne's had enough...
Mleh—

W-wait, Blaine!! Please, just a few more minutes!!

I just figured out how to mix the paints, so—

Frederick! I said brushes down.

You know I wish for your victory, but we have to abide by the rules.

And part of being a prince means to know when to stand down... even if it means accepting a loss.

...

...No...

The painting portion of the competition is over.

Now in order to determine the winner and the loser, it's time...

...in front of the judge.

All I wanted to do was come here to talk to Gwen...
and now I'm about to lose the right to ever talk to her again?!
I **know**. I'm not supposed to listen to those negative thoughts.
I'm supposed to clear them away and rely on my willpower...

...but I don't have any left!!
The judge is now ready to review both contestants' portraits.

Laverne will then bless the winner's painting...
Z Z Z
...and **crush** the loser's.

On the count of three, the curtain will be lifted.

glance
One...
This sucks...

Two...
...?
snore~

I'm just a failure...

Three!
Whoosh~

Oooooohhh...

It was a bit rushed, but I hope you'll find this portrait acceptable, Your Honor.
Okay...But Frederick's portrait, on the other hand...
...Is that even paint...?!

Wheeze

Ohhh, man, this isn't even a contest! We messed up big time!
It's okay. I trust Laverne!
One pretty painting isn't going to make her forget where her loyalty truly lies!
Let's see what she does with Leopold's portrait!
step
step
Stare-
...**That's** her blessing for the winner's portrait?
SMOOOCH-

Welp, so much for loyalty...
Uh-oh... does that mean...?

STOMP

Stomp
Stomp
Stomp
...Laverne's going to crush Frederick's painting and declare him the loser?!

KICK!
Sigh...This is it. Goodbye, Gwen...

BONK

WAIT!!!

I...I love this...

I don't care what the verdict is—
I'll forfeit the match if you'll allow me to have this painting!

W-wait... what? Y-you **want** that...?!
I mean, you can just take it. You don't have to—

OW!!!
We accept your forfeit!!!
Shhhh, Frederick...
shake

AAAGH–
Frederick!! Frederick!!
toss

Yawn Aww, boys' duels are so cute...
clap
clap

step
step

Um... hey, Leopold? I-I'm sorry I called you a serpent.
You're definitely not...
...Are you sure you didn't lie about wanting my portrait to help me win?
Though I'm not sure why you would do that...

grip
In the frequent words of my butler...
"You can pry this portrait from my cold, dead hands."
You'd better keep up your end of the wager...and ask Gwendolyn to the gala.
I-I'm going to right now...

My brothers just gave me some advice...
It's all about hiding that ticket in a gift and surprising her with it!
nod

Well...the only advice I want to give you is that...
you're going to need a lot more grit to go after what you want, Frederick...
...especially with Gwendolyn...as well as the formidable people surrounding her.

Formidable... shiny...people.
shudder-

Do you really have to leave now? Can't everyone stay for dinner, at least?

I'm sorry. We have to get Frederick home now. He has one important thing left to do, though.

FREDERICK'S WILLPOWER METER
Okay...you're exhausted, you've been through a lot today...and this is the hardest part.
But just dig up every last drop of determination you have left, and you'll make it through!
Here I go...
step
step
Oh...the ticket!
...So that's what this is about...
I'm glad we didn't spoil the surprise and tell Gwen...
...when we got our tickets to the gala!
WIN

Yes, Frederick?
Um, uhhh...
I-it was nice to see you again, Gwen. B-but I want to, uh...
I can feel everyone staring at us...!

Oh!

Your bookmark was still inside! Here you go!
It looks important...

Now!
Gwen... will y—?

She...
She doesn't even think the ticket is for her...
It's like the idea could never even cross her mind!

Okay. No problem. Just explain...!
Come on, say something...
sputter
WILLPOWER METER:
EMPTY

Hurry! You're making her wait!
You're making everyone wait! Just say **anything**!

Oh, thanks.

...
step
step

Uhh, see ya later, Your Highnesses!
W-Wait! Frederick!
dash–
I should have just kicked his butt...

Though to be fair, he couldn't have gotten very far anyhow...
given Gwendolyn's current mindset.
After all, as I said before...

...one can only accept love from others...
...to the degree that they allow it within themselves.

step
step
H-hey, Gwen...
Um...

How do I put this *delicately*...?
You know... sometimes it's not the book...
it's what's **inside** the book that matters.

Huh? Wait...
Wh-what did you just say?
Where have I heard that before?!

It's what's inside of the book that matters.
...How does Maria know what my fortune cookie said?!

Clop
Clop

It's okay, Frederick.
How about we come back next weekend or so...
and give it one more try?!

You'll feel better after some sleep, some restrategizing...
and a shower. Lots of showers...

At the very least, you should be proud of yourself.
I've never seen you take on something that challenging...
and stick with it all the way through.
pat

I'm impressed. And I know Father will feel the same way.

Wait...where's Laverne?!! And the llamakärt?!
Father will kill me if I don't bring both of them back!
Oh. Don't worry, that's all taken care of.
Lance was intrigued and wanted to give it a spin...
huff
huff
...
This thing's frickin' awesome!!
More to come, following this interlude...

Jamie's Dream
Okay, children!
That's it for *Hansel and Gretel*! Time for bed now.
Sweet dreams!
Hansel & Gretel
Okay, Dad!
Z
Z
Z

I...I think we're lost in the forest!
I'm really hungry, Sis...
Wait...is this a trail of marshmallow bunnies?
munch
munch
Whoa!! Is that...?

Mmm, it's a gingerbread house!!
Chomp
Chomp
Oh my, I've lured in such a pretty child!
Yes! Get nice and plump before I eat you!
Hello, my pretty!
Do you like my house that I made entirely by hand out of delicious treats?
I do!! I taste gingerbread, frosting, and a little loneliness.
Um... what?
I taste resentment toward your peers for not reciprocating your friendship.
chew
chew

Well...sure. I mean, I always attend their craft nights because that's just what friends do.
But whenever I hold a dinner party, no one can make time.
Chomp
Chomp
nod
But if I say anything, they'll just think I'm insensitive.
Shelly has to take the kids to mock witch trial and Carol has fibromyalgia.
pat
Wow...I've never said any of that out loud before.
It's obvious now that I just need to be honest with them and appreciate the time we have together.
Thanks for listening.

Bye...
Whoosh~
shiver
nom
nom

Chapter 7

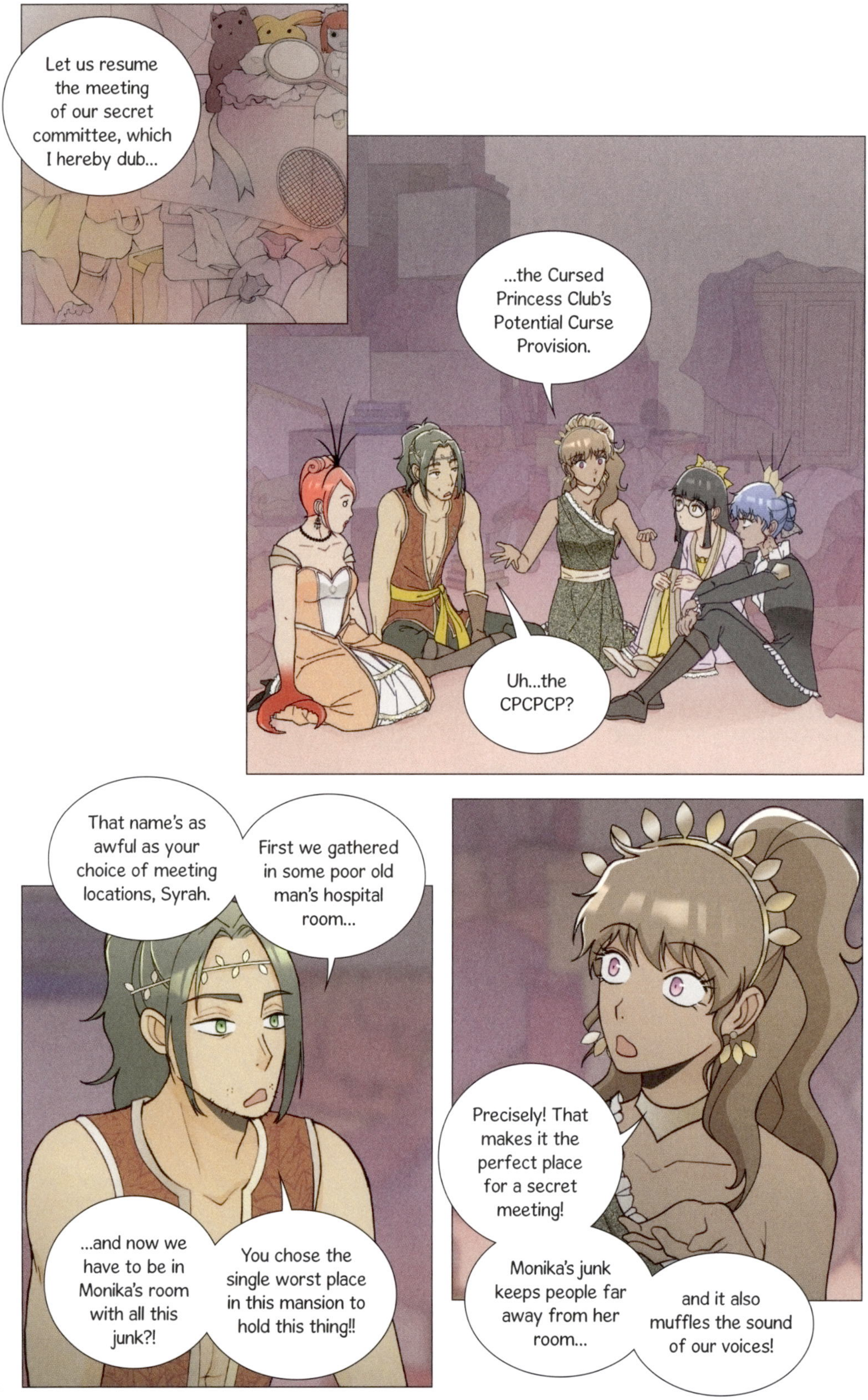

Let us resume the meeting of our secret committee, which I hereby dub...

...the Cursed Princess Club's Potential Curse Provision.

Uh...the CPCPCP?

Heyyy, it's not junk...
Um, sorry, but can we keep this short?

I know I was the one who started this whole inquiry into Gwen's potential curse and all, but...
...we also now have a much more important threat...
of a member potentially dying in the next few weeks, according to Nell's premonition.
And I think I figured out what it's going to be from.

we are here
NEW MOON
I found a chart that shows this month's moon phases.
Here we are now. And there's when the new moon will happen in a few weeks.
That's pretty much exactly when, um, my time of the month starts.
And you guys know what that means...

...I think I'm going to kill someone again in my cursed form.

I believe we have plenty of time to avoid this tragedy.
We just have to make absolutely sure that I stay locked in the barn this time.

...Right...
Hey, feel bad for her all you want...
but at least she's not in danger of pushing up daisies right now.

Okay, well let's cut to the chase, then.
I heard from Gwen that her father goes on these mysterious expeditions from time to time.
That **could** be a clue to something...

Perhaps...though that doesn't give us very much information to sink our claws into.
What did she say about her mother?

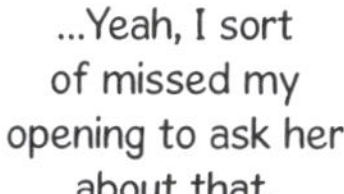

...Yeah, I sort of missed my opening to ask her about that.
But Gwen's coming to the club in a few hours, so I definitely won't miss it again today!
Maybe we can—

Hey, wait a minute...
grab
Monika, this is my favorite nail polish that I've been trying to find for weeks...
Have you been stealing things from my room again?!

Whoa...yeah, and this is my lute over here!
You can't take this!!
I was **gonna** get to learning to play this... someday.

And Monika, these are my old molted claws...!
If I knew you were a fan, I would have brought my back catalog by earlier...

I thought we had a talk about not stealing from your clubmates anymore.
But... but...

Come on, Monika!
You need to give everyone's stuff back!!
...

Meanwhile, outside the CPC Mansion...
Okay, **this** time kick the hacky back to me, Jolie!
We're playing hacky sack, not cornhole!!
kick

Oh! Hey, Gwen! I thought you weren't coming until later...
because of your fancy portrait painting session!
step
step
Are those more baked treats?

Yeah...I get the feeling our portrait artist is wary of being in our palace any longer.
He finished it really quickly today and said it just has to dry now before we can see the final product.
So I thought I'd bake some donuts and come here early!
Do either of you know where Curtis is? I brought him the recipe.

Um, I think he's busy at the moment.
Prez mentioned they'd be at the barn replacing all of the locks that were melted.
Oh... R-right...

honk
chomp

Um, on that note...How has Renée been?
Aurelia was her best friend in the club. And now she's...gone.
Has Renée reached out to her?

Nah, I think she's actually more angry at Aurelia than anyone else here.
You know, some people hold their best friends to higher standards and all that...

Oh...
Um, I've been wondering about something lately...
How often are members banished from the CPC?

Hmm...I've never actually seen Prez banish anyone else once they were in the club...
I think that's because she's really strict in her scouting process before she brings anyone here.
Yeah, it sounds like she has to weed through a bunch of duds.
I guess the spiders don't always give her the best leads...

...Like the time they led Prez and Curtis into a cave of cursed vampire princesses...
SHRIEK~!!
AAAHHH! DEFINITELY NOT A GOOD FIT FOR THE CLUB!!!
Even if the potential recruit won't be a safety threat to all of us...
she still vets them to see if they will treat each of us with kindness and respect.
A club full of cursed princesses?! How many of them are uggos, though? Be honest, Mr. President!
For the last time, **I'M** the president, and Curtis is my butler...
And she doesn't just look out for the women but for the safety of the few guys in our club as well...
Oh, good, do we each get our own male slave?
Tell yours to grovel right now for all the disgusting things his gender has ever done.
Whoa, whoa, Curtis isn't a slave!
Syrah barely passed that last test, by the way...

I see...
Um, just out of curiosity...
do you think Prez would ever change her mind after she banished someone?

Hah, yeah right.
Once Prez gets angry like that, no one can change her mind about anything.

Yeah...
Prez is really amazing. She's a great leader, strong...
Confusingly hot...

...but no one's perfect.
Prez has a strong stubborn side to her...
especially when it comes to people's safety in this club.

Wait...Are you saying that you want Aurelia back in the club?!
Even after what she tried to do to you?!
Are you out of your mind?!

I-I don't think she meant to physically hurt me...

And I feel like I understand her frustrations.

She's right. I'm not even cursed, but you guys let me into your club.

I relied too much on your help when other people deserved it more.

Gwen, everyone here deserves to have help, including you.

We were happy to help you because you opened up to us with your problems.

But we can't know unless people ask for it. And Aurelia didn't.

Good.
Now let me dote on those donuts and help you carry them to the kitchen...
grab
step
step

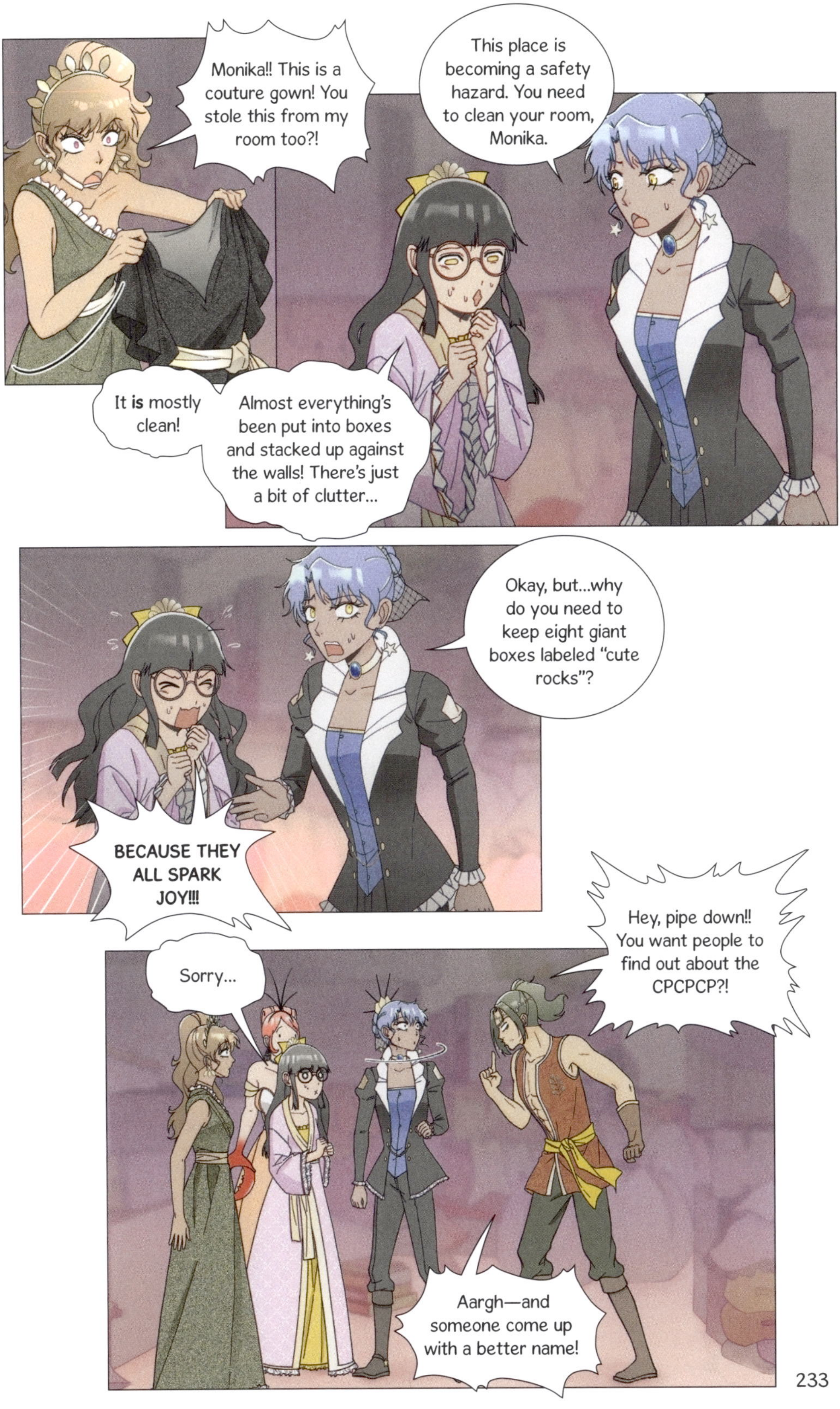

Monika!! This is a couture gown! You stole this from my room too?!
This place is becoming a safety hazard. You need to clean your room, Monika.
It **is** mostly clean!
Almost everything's been put into boxes and stacked up against the walls! There's just a bit of clutter...
Okay, but...why do you need to keep eight giant boxes labeled "cute rocks"?
BECAUSE THEY ALL SPARK JOY!!!
Sorry...
Hey, pipe down!! You want people to find out about the CPCPCP?!
Aargh—and someone come up with a better name!

#@!
chatter
yell
What's going on in Monika's room? Usually, no one is in there.
Sounds like a party...
step
step

Party? Do you think they would like some dessert?

Hmm...Let's find out...!
knock
knock

Eep...!!

twist

Swing!
Hey, guys!! Whatcha doin' in here?

Uhhh, **nothing**...!!

Oh crap, no...!!
SLAP!
Must...hold... it in...

Hrrnngghh—

POW!

SLAM!

CRASH!

GROAN-

Ughhh, I hate this game...

I finally have a free afternoon, and my Gwennie-pie is gone at her extracurricular study again!

The **audacity** of this fancy-schmancy princess college to assume education is more important than game night!

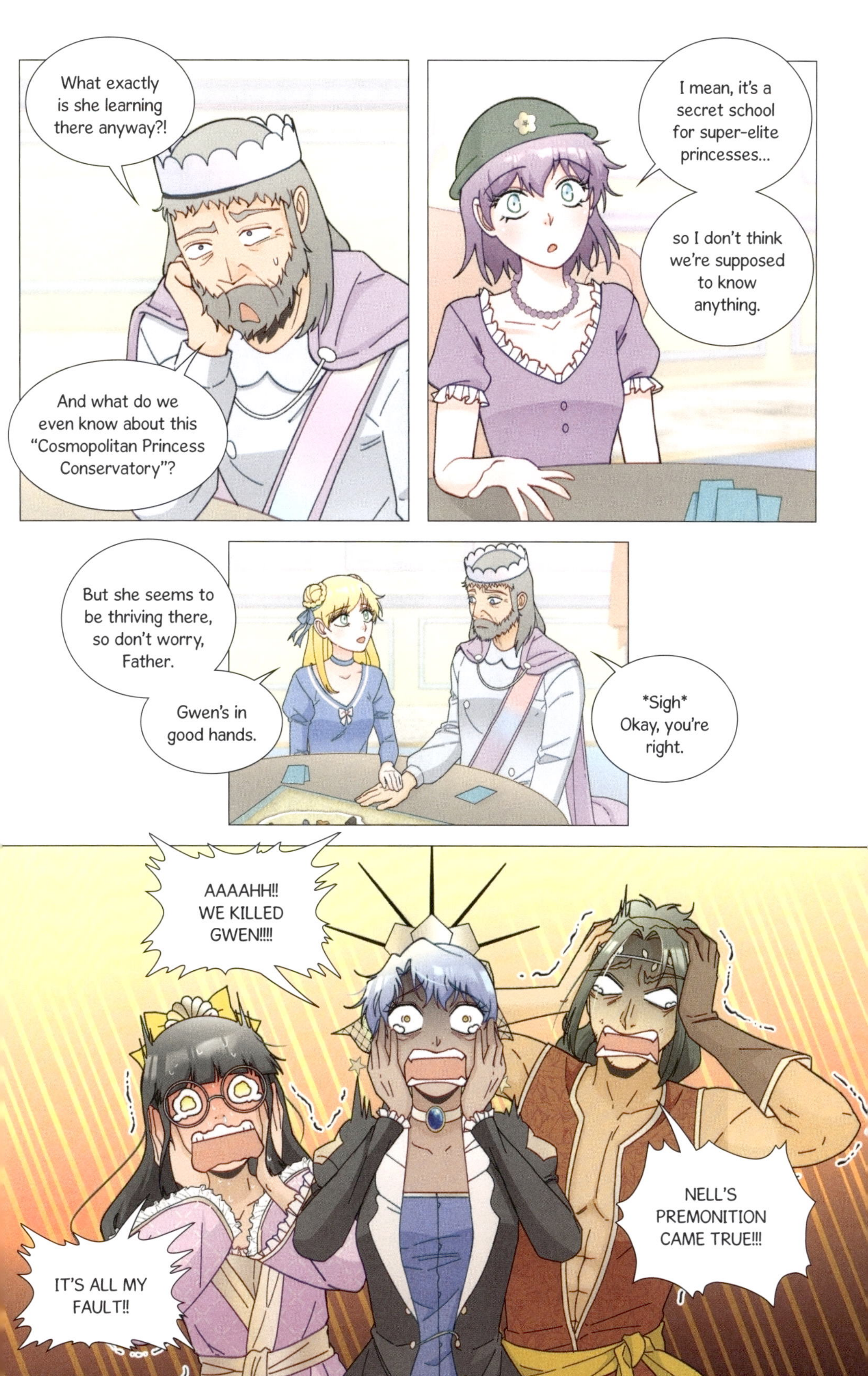
What exactly is she learning there anyway?!
And what do we even know about this "Cosmopolitan Princess Conservatory"?
I mean, it's a secret school for super-elite princesses...
so I don't think we're supposed to know anything.
But she seems to be thriving there, so don't worry, Father.
Gwen's in good hands.
Sigh Okay, you're right.
AAAAHH!! WE KILLED GWEN!!!!
NELL'S PREMONITION CAME TRUE!!!
IT'S ALL MY FAULT!!

POOF!!
Gwen...
sob
It all happened in a flash, just like Nell said.

Um...I-I'm fine, guys.
...Huh?

sniffle
Gwen?! ...Is that you?!
B-but how could you survive all that stuff falling on you?!

squish
Oh, Monika's stuffed animal collection landed on me first. It kind of just felt like a big hug.
And it formed a little padded dome in here.
But I don't think I can climb out without everything caving in.

O-okay! Just hold tight and we'll dig you out as fast as possible!
It'll take a while, though...
There's just so much crap here, MONIKA!!!

burrow—

step
step
...?
What's going on in here?

Oh, hey, Nell!! Great news—
Your premonition didn't come true!!!
All this stuff fell on Gwen, but she didn't get hurt.
So we can all stop worrying now!

...Hrmm...
CRUNCH
Mm, nope. That wasn't it.
Wh-what do you mean? That wasn't the premonition?
How can you know?!
How can you just bite into an ice pop like that?
Trust me, I'll know. If and when it happens, I'll feel a jolt throughout my body, and—
AAAGH!!

GASP
Was that it?!

...No. Brain freeze.
Oh.

Well, I guess I'm glad you're safe, Gwen... again...
step
step

So wait...Does that mean Nell's premonition could still happen...?

rustle
dig

pop!
Monika!!

Caw-!!
relief~

POOF!!
Oh, Gwen!! I'm so sorry!!!
You almost died because of all my dumb junk!!
squeeze

It's not junk!
I've been looking around, and there are a lot of nice things in here!!

Right?!! You understand me, Gwen!!
This is my treasure trove!
There's no better feeling than to just fly in my room in any direction...
and be surrounded by pretty, shiny things from floor to ceiling!

It's one of the few things that comforts me when I'm anxious, and I feel like everything's too much.

Too much?

Yeah...Don't you think everything in life is scary, Gwen?
Every second is just waiting to be filled with bad feelings, embarrassments, or scary people...

That's what it's felt like since I was kidnapped by that stupid creepy wizard...
who turned me into a bird when I was little.

Yeah...the more I learn about the world...
it does seem like it can be really scary sometimes.

So then why is everyone able to eventually go out there like it's no big deal...
except for me?
I still feel like I can't ever grow up from being that little girl.

It's the same with my curse. The potion the doctors gave me was supposed to make me a normal girl again...
not some mutant who turns into a crow whenever I'm stressed.
But after a while, they just all gave up and said they didn't know how to help me anymore.
And since then, I've just been...**stuck**.
And all I've done since then is make a big mess for myself...
and for everyone around me.

I can't stop feeling anxious...
so I can't stop turning into a bird.
And so I can't be the princess that I'm supposed to be for my kingdom.
I can't accomplish any of the goals I want to in life.
Oh, like opening your own jewelry store, right?
I remember that was your wish when we made Abbi's potion.
The paper necklace you made me was amazing! It's hanging on my jewelry stand.

B-but...I thought you said you didn't like it...
What? No, I love it—!
Gwennn—!

The jewelry thing is a pipe dream.
I'd be happy if I could just do normal things, like have a pet...o-or go on dates...
but I'll never even be able to do that.

Um...there's something I've been meaning to tell you.
When everything was happening at the barn the other day...

...and Aurelia was yelling at me...
...I remember you stood up and defended me...
while I was too scared to say anything the entire time. And I don't even have a curse that would turn me into a bird.

I-I mean, yeah, it was super scary...
but I didn't want her to hurt you.
And if I turned into a bird, I wouldn't have been able to do anything.

Well, I've been wanting to say thank you...
And that, I dunno...
...I think you're a lot braver now than you think.

...

M-maybe I could try a little harder.
But...is there some way I can grow up...
and still keep all my cute, pretty things?

Um, I **think** so...
Maybe just not the things that don't belong to you, though?
Hmm...
Rumble
Rumble

AH!! We finally broke through!!
You're free now!!

Hey, Monika. Gwen's right about you being tougher now than you think.
I wish there was a magic cure that could fix us completely, like we were told to believe...

...but we shouldn't have to wait until we've fixed everything to feel whole.
We should all take more time to admire who we are right now, with all the pieces we've gathered so far.

And you know, Monika...
if you give back my stuff, you can always visit it in my room, as long as it stays there.
Yeah, same here, girl! Come by anytime!
Just don't open my bottom drawer...
And don't say I didn't warn you...

Also, if you can keep this room less cluttered...
I think it could be safe for you to have a pet in here someday.

REALLY??!! I want a pet **so bad**!!!
I-I'll clean everything up, then!!
I just don't know where to start. There's too much stuff—

It's okay! You don't need to rush.
If you'd like, we can just sit and hang out with you...
and we can take it one step at a time.

...Okay.

How do you feel about this set of teaspoons?

They're pretty!! I wanna keep them!

Okay! I'll put them in this pile.

What about these shoes?

Um...I like them, but they belong to Abbi. Sorry.

Thanks, Monika.

Come on, guys, stop looking. It's making Monika feel uncomfortable—

AAAAHH, DON'T LOOK AT THAT!!!!

OMG, so adorable. I can't take it.

AAAAHH!!
roll
Um... speaking of moms...
D-does your mom like things like baby books, Gwen?

Oh...She passed away when I was three, so I guess I don't really know.

...!!
I-I'm sorry. I didn't mean to bring up any painful memories...

No, it's okay!! It's not painful for me at all.
I don't have any memories of her, actually.

Well, there's one thing I remember...
My earliest memory is when my mom was holding me.
All I can recall is feeling... warm and... **glowy**.

She sounds lovely...

I'm sure she was...though I don't actually know what she looked like.
Papa had all the paintings of her covered up and hidden away deep in the palace after her death.
He said that just the sight of her portrait will make him weep for months on end.
So we never speak of our mom because we don't wanna make Papa sad.

H-huh?! But—

Gasp~!
HOLD UP, MONIKA.
Did you steal **Saffron's** baby book out of his room too?!!
WHAT?!! NOOOOO!!!!
Hahaha... ha...
Psst, are you thinking what I'm thinking?
Mm-hmm...
That if the CPCPCP wants any more answers about Gwen...
...WE NEED TO GET INSIDE THAT PALACE.

A few days later...

Gwennie?
Gwennie-pie, are you in the kitchen?

Yes, Papa! I'm right here! What's wrong?!

What's wrong? Absolutely **nothing** is wrong! It couldn't be more right, actually!!
Leopold finished your portrait!
Y-Your Majesty, please be careful with that!

Look, sweetie! It's you!!!
It's **perfectly** you, in every way!
...!
...Perfectly me...
...in every way?

That's right, Gwendolyn.
And once it's hung up here on your palace walls...
it will serve as a daily reminder of your stately beaut—

Oh, this painting won't be hung in our palace!
It won't?

Nope! But on that note...
I should probably handle preparations for its shipment now.
Leopold, I'll be sure to leave a glowing review for your incredible work.
I also had Molly prepare your payment of one ginormous sack of gems. It'll be waiting for you at the door whenever you're ready.
shake
Th-thank you very much, Your Majesty.

Well, Gwendolyn, I apologize for barging in on you here.
But I do want to say a proper goodbye before I take my leave.
skip~
I had a truly wonderful time getting to know you over these last few days.

Me too. Will we get to see you again?

Oh, well of course. I **am** your family's royal portrait artist now.

But I have a hunch we'll be running into each other at an event sometime this season...

if that little worm can pull himself together in time.

Sooo...
Here it is! I hope you like it!!
Eat me, boy—
Gag
Uggghh...
W-wow...that looks very, uh... frosted.
Oh, oops!! No! Not that one!!
push

This is yours!
It's bread made with sage and rosemary...
since I recall you saying you aren't a fan of sweet foods.

You baked that for me?
It looks amazing.

Actually, I have something I'd like to give to you too...
I was helping Bart clean up the portrait room, and I came upon some sketches.
pull

And seeing as how I was wrong about where your portrait will be residing...
I'm glad to at least be able to give you this.

It's a sketch
of Jamie and
me...!

Gwendolyn,
you asked me to
help you learn to
love yourself without
relying on anyone
else...
and I'm
sorry to say I
wasn't able to
do much.
But the truth
is you're never
fully alone. Your
friends and
family are always
with you...
in memories,
in objects,
and in art.

So if you ever
find yourself
alone...
and in doubt
of what you
deserve...
...then I hope
you'll see this sketch
of your brother's
face as he looks at
you...
for that is the
face of someone
who truly believes
you deserve the
world.
Thank you,
Leopold.

You know, I actually have to thank Prince Jamie.

His expression that day made me realize something important too.

I always prided myself on my unique perspectives on beauty.

I felt like I could help shake society out of its simpleminded tastes.

And when I first saw your brother, all I could see was the epitome of everything I despised...

someone who loved to bask shamelessly in his sugary-sweet looks and steal everyone's attention.

But when I saw Jamie actually walk over and speak to you...

...it was like a light shone down...

and I was able to properly see him for the first time as he truly was.

I saw someone who wasn't afraid to love and protect his sisters...

in the most bizarrely fearless way possible.

And, frankly, that's undeniably beautiful in my book.

I realized that my values were ultimately just as shortsighted as society's.
Perhaps beauty isn't a stagnant thing that can be judged in one glance.
And therefore...
perhaps I was wrong about your brother's appearance after all.

NOT that that pink demon shall ever hear those words come out of my mouth.

Well, if you would like to say goodbye to Jamie before you go...
I was just about to bring this to him for his lunch!

That **vile structure**...
is Jamie's **lunch**?!

It **is** the type of monstrosity only he is capable of consuming...
B-but that doesn't mean you should indulge him like that, Gwendolyn!
Anyone who eats that will drop dead from a sugar coma!
Ohhh, that's **just** what that little demon wants, isn't it...
It's not enough that his face won't stop haunting my dreams!
He would be **delighted** to do it as an actual ghost!!
Well, if he thinks I'll allow him that satisfaction, he's **wrong**!
I'll stuff him full of vegetables and micronutrients so he lives forever!!!
grab
Gwendolyn, I'm borrowing your produce!!

Oh my...

What's going on here?

Oh! Jamie's an accomplished food critic, and lots of chefs stop by to have him taste their dishes.
Have you ever come across any of his articles in the magazines you've painted for?

Hmm. Um...maybe? I'm not particularly interested in articles other than my own.

Jamie eats a lot during these sessions...
but he likes it when I bring him a familiar snack between his tastings.
He says it helps refresh his palate and his mind.
You know, because of his amazing ability to taste the emotions of the people who prepare his food.

Sorry, what did you just say?

Oh—sorry, I should explain.
Jamie's spent his entire life tasting everything he could get his hands on.
Eventually, he even became able to taste the feelings of the people who prepare the things he eats. Pretty neat, right?

...Noooo...

...Nooooo...
clink
No, no, no, no, nonono...
Excuse me! Pardon me!
Hey! No cutting, pal!
dash—
Ah~
DON'T EAT—
CHOMP
—that.
Mmm!! Did you make this, Leopold?
It's really great! I'm impressed by the invigorating splash of lemon and tarragon.

I-is that all?
You didn't, um, taste **it**?
Taste what?

That...um...
...I-I don't think you're hideous. Er...
You're actually, maybe...*cough*... b-beautiful.

Oh...well, yeah, but that flavor's in everything.

munch~
...

After Gwen's portrait was completed, life seemed to calm down for everyone for a short while.

Time was spent on such things as hanging new artwork...

That was, until one night about a week later...
CLOUDS...
THE CLOUDS...
THE CLOUDS ARE CONVERGING TOMORROW...
But not before one final interlude...

Lorena's Dream
And that's the end of *Jack and the Beanstalk*. Go on up to bed now, kids!
Jack & the Beanstalk
Okay! Goodnight, Daddy!
snore~

Wow, it's morning already?
stretch!
I wonder how high this goes...
Hmm, that's odd...
Giant flowers do grow while I sleep, but this one turned out **REALLY** big!
Whoa, there's a palace up here!!

...And there's a giant man inside!
Z
Z
z
step
step
Hubba-hubba.
Hmm, that waffle looks pretty good too.
...I haven't had breakfast yet.
He **is** asleep. So maybe I'll just take that last bite...
Z
Z
z
Chomp
snort
Huh...?
Uh-oh...

HEY!! I was saving that last bite of waffle!!
GET BACK HERE!!
AAAH!!
Slide~
WHACK!
YAH!

Whoooa!!
SLAM
Come to mama, you hot giant.
So hot...so heavy...
The End.

Match THE PRINCESS

with THE CURSE

4
I have my own handy built-in storage

2
Just trying to get to the prom

8
Some of my best friends are spiders

5
I'm a back stabber - or should I say 'melter'?"

7
Am I telling the truth? Who nose?

6
I just want to sea my one true love

9
The zipper is the solution and not the curse

ANSWER KEY ON FINAL PAGE

The Cursed

GRAPHIC NOVEL DISCUSSION QUESTIONS

- How do the images and text work together to communicate the story?
- Would this story be as meaningful if it was not written in graphic novel format?
- How, if at all, do the characters in the graphic novel change throughout the text? What does the creator LambCat do to show these changes?
- How would this story change if you covered the pictures and only read the text?
- Why do you think the author chose to tell this story in graphic novel format?
- How do you think the pictures helped you visualize the characters?
- Why do you think some panels are different sizes in the book?
- Describe how the text and pictures work together to create a meaningful part of the story?

CURSED PRINCESS CLUB QUESTIONS

- Lambcat, the creator, didn't create Cursed Princess Club as a graphic novel. Are you new to reading graphic novels/comics? If so:
  - Did you enjoy the experience?
  - What did you like/dislike, compared to the reading experience of a prose novel?

Princess Book Club

- If you aren't a new graphic novel reader, are you a WEBTOON reader, and did you read Cursed Princess Club in the Webtoon scrolling format? If so...
  - How does this graphic novel differ from the Webtoon?
  - Did you have a preference of Webtoon over Graphic Novel?
  - Did anything change in the storytelling from Webtoon to Graphic Novel, in your mind?
- Have you read other graphic novels? How would you compare this experience?
- Graphic novels often use the "page turn" to land a joke, or pique the readers' curiosity to turn the page, or to plan a big reveal. Do you see examples of the "page turn" in Cursed Princess Club? Discuss

BODY POSITIVITY/ NEGATIVITY QUESTIONS

- Gwendolyn seems to be suffering from negative body image issues.
  - Do you think she's actually suffering from negative body issues, or a curse?
  - What other characters in the book, male and female, deal with negative body issues? List and discuss.
  - Which characters do you think will overcome/are overcoming their negative issues?
  - Which characters are not overcoming their negative body issues?
- Negative body issues are very common in today's society. If you feel comfortable sharing, please tell the group how you've suffered from any negative body issues.
- Go around the group, saying one or two things you like about each other in a positive way. It doesn't have to be a physical characteristic!

LambCat is a small, omnivorous, and easily frightened creature who has burrowed deep into the Pacific Northwest to draw comics and make music. They can be lured out by Bill Evans records and frosted animal crackers.

Read the original on www.WEBTOON.com